V

EONO

(Book Six)

A HOLLY ST. JAMES ROMANTIC MYSTERY

EONO

(Book Six)

•

GEORGETTE
LIVINGSTON

AVALON BOOKS
THOMAS BOUREGY AND COMPANY, INC.
401 LAFAYETTE STREET
NEW YORK, NEW YORK 10003

PRINTED IN THE UNITED STATES OF AMERICA
ON ACID-FREE PAPER
BY HADDON CRAFTSMEN, SCRANTON, PENNSYLVANIA

For the real Cindy and Danny, with much love.

Also a special thanks to Lucy Fuchino, my Hawaiian friend who has been a tremendous help.

Glossary

'AE: Yes
AHUI HO: Until we meet again
AIKANE: Friend
ALOHA: Love, farewell, welcome
ALOHA AU IA OE: I love you
ALOHA NUI LOA: Much love
AUWE: Alas, woe is me!
HALE: House
HAOLE: Caucasian
HAOLEKANE: Caucasian man
HAOLEWAHINE: Caucasian female
HAU'OLI: Rejoice
HAUPIA: Gelatin dessert made from coconut
HOLOHOLO: Go for a walk, ride, sail
HOLOMU'U: Fitted ankle-length dress
KAMA'AINA: Native-born
KANE: Man, husband
KAUKAU: Food
KEIKI: Child or grown child
KULEANA: By extension, used to designate somebody's area
LEI: Garland, wreath
MAIKA'I: Good, fine
MAKE: Dead
MALIHINI: Stranger, newcomer
MAUNA: Mountain
MUUMUU: Long or short loose-fitting dress
NANI: Beautiful, lovely
OHANA: Family
'ONO: Delicious, tasty
PIKAKE: Jasmine
PILAU: Putrid
PILIKIA: Trouble
PUPULE: Crazy
UKU: Type of fish
WAHINE: Female, wife
WIKIWIKI: Fast, hurry

Chapter One

Holly stood at the railing, and lifted her face to the spray of salt water as the *Sea Breeze* edged closer to the harbor that rimmed the historical waterfront town of Lahaina. Beyond, the towering West Maui Mountains seemed to reach for the sky, shrouded only at the top by puffy, gray-and-white misty clouds.

The cruise over from the island of Kauai had been a delightful experience, made possible by Logan's expert yachtsmanship, and by the vessel herself, a sleek, lovely craft called a "motor sailer/cruiser" because she was equipped with three diesel engines as well as white, billowy sails.

1

It hadn't been a spur-of-the-moment decision to celebrate their first anniversary on Maui, where they'd spent their honeymoon. Holly and Logan West had been talking about it for weeks, just waiting for a free block of time in their busy schedules. And although they had planned to take a large group of friends (along with Tutu, the dear little lady— a *kama'aina*, or native-born islander—they had hired as a housekeeper), only newlyweds Cindy and Danny Wells had been able to get away for the length of time necessary to make the trip, and enjoy a week on the "valley island."

Tutu had announced up front she wasn't a very good sailor, but was willing to give it a try. At the moment she was in the salon, giving thanks to *Na Make o Ka Hai*, goddess of the sea, that they all made it to shore.

Cindy stood with Holly on the deck, excitement clearly etched on her face, and admitted, "Well, I guess I can tell you now, now that we're here safe and sound. I'm not a good sailor, either, and if it hadn't been for the fact that Danny was so excited about this trip, I would have declined. Not that I'm prone to seasickness or anything; it just makes me feel claustrophobic. You know, being surrounded by miles and miles of water, with no way off the boat except to row a tiny dinghy, or swim. But, oh, I'm so glad we came! So far, everything has been fabulous, and just the thought of spending some quality time on this romantic island with Danny . . . Well, I suppose I'm sounding like a dippy newlywed, but . . .'' She ran a hand through her windblown, coffee-colored hair. "Umm, I think we're going to take Logan's suggestion, and spend our nights on the *Sea Breeze* instead of in one of the rooms above Stump's bar."

Holly smiled at her longtime friend. "Logan only suggested it because Stump is renovating the bar, and things will probably be in a bit of a mess. He also thought it would give the two of you more privacy, and you'll have the well-stocked galley at your disposal, too, in the event you decide to hibernate for a few days."

Cindy sighed dreamily. "Well, that certainly sounds tempting, but we'll have to settle for romantic nights because Danny has a long list of things he wants to do. He's never been to Maui, and he wants to see *everything*. I tried to tell him if we had a month, he wouldn't be able to see it all, but he seems determined to try."

"That's the way I felt when we were here on our honeymoon," Holly admitted. "But our plans sort of went awry."

"Uh-huh, because you got involved in a murder case. Well, I'm not an adventuresome private investigator like you, Holly, and Danny isn't a semiretired federal agent like Logan, so even if a dead body happens to drop at our feet . . ."

"What's all this about a dead body?" Danny asked, joining them at the rail.

Cindy squeezed her husband's hand. "We were talking about Holly and Logan's honeymoon that turned into a wild and woolly murder case. I was about to say, no dead bodies allowed on this trip."

Danny was a handsome young man with auburn hair, blue, blue eyes, and a sprinkling of freckles across his nose. He looked like he was fresh out of college, when in fact he was the director of security at one of the major hotels on Kauai, and had been for several years. "No dead bodies allowed," he murmured, kissing Cindy's cheek. "Just lots of love, good food, and island adventure. I'm also looking forward to meeting Stump Tanner. He sounds like one colorful character.''

Holly grinned. ''To say the least. Visualize every pirate you've ever seen in the movies, roll them all into one, and you have Stump Tanner. Tan, craggy face, white hair that he wears in a buzz cut, a gold front tooth, gold earring in one ear, and of course his infamous peg leg. He's really into movies, too, especially old ones, and can name them and the years they were made without even blinking. The last time we were here, he had a large photo of his favorite old-time actress above the bar. He won it in some kind of a contest involving Coca-Cola bottle caps.''

Danny's blue eyes twinkled. ''Fay Wray? I was a kid the first time I saw the original *King Kong* on TV, and I'm still in love.''

Holly smiled when Cindy gave Danny a healthy poke in the ribs, and said, ''You're about ten years off. It's Hedy Lamarr. Before I got to know him, I thought Stump's appearance and deportment might be an act. But believe me, it isn't. He is exactly who he is. A rugged sailor and adventurer, who finally decided to put down roots after traveling all over the world. And lucky for us, he chose the islands. Logan met him while he was over here on police business, and their friendship escalated from there. He lost his leg to a shark in Australian waters, by the way, but you'd better not feel sorry for him. He gets around as well as any man with two good legs, and the word sympathy isn't in his vocabulary. He can be a bit intimidating, but his heart is as big as his smile.''

Danny said, ''He sounds like just the kind of guy who would own a bar on the waterfront.''

''Actually, it's much more than a bar, Danny. Stump serves food, too, and brings in an island combo every night for the enjoyment of his customers.''

''So, it's more like a supper club,'' Cindy said.

''Well, not exactly that, either. It's too rustic. It has a marred plank floor, cane tables with wooden slab tops that Stump encourages his customers to carve up with their initials, a high beamed ceiling with a creaking ceiling fan, and he caters to a lot of locals who just like to sit around and talk. It's their home away from home, and they all adore Stump.''

Danny said, ''Sounds like a joint befitting

the owner. I take it he's a confirmed bachelor? I mean, with a salty career like that . . .''

"He is now. He was married four times, and the last wife cleaned him out financially. I know, you have to wonder how he had time for one wife, let alone four.''

Danny chuckled. "I'll bet he has a few tales to tell—'' He broke off, and cupped a hand to his ear. "Listen to the silence. Tutu has stopped chanting. Do you suppose she's gotten up the courage to open her eyes? If so, and she's seen the dock . . .''

"Tutu has seen the dock, and can feel her heart beating again,'' Tutu said, padding out on deck. "And Tutu can now smile. Tutu is smiling, see? Good show, o' wot?''

Plump, gray-haired, and adorable, Tutu's smile was as bright as her colorful, oversized muumuu. "And your smile is a wonderful sight to see,'' Holly said, giving her a hug. "Now, aren't you glad you came?''

Tutu smoothed down the muumuu with her pudgy hands and nodded. '' *'Ae*, for now. *Kane* Logan is a good sailor. Came through the water *wikiwiki*.''

Danny had gone to help Logan moor the boat, and Cindy pointed at the dock. "That *has* to be Stump Tanner! Over there, standing near the pile of fishing nets.''

"It's Stump," Holly said, waving both arms.

Tutu clucked her tongue. "That *haolekane* looks crusty like an old crab, but the smile is like *aikane*. That is *maika'i*. Good."

Holly said, "It's *very* good, Tutu, but remember what I said. No matter what goes on in the bar, especially in the kitchen, Tonoa is the cook, and what he says is gospel." She looked at Cindy and shrugged. "Just thought I'd better set down some ground rules. Tutu is a very good cook and has the habit of speaking her mind, especially when it comes to food and its preparation. And considering Tonoa is a bit of a grump, he wouldn't take too kindly to her opinions, should she find something not to her liking."

Tutu gave Holly a wry smile. "Tutu will find everything *'ono*, very tasty, even if it is *pilau*."

Cindy raised a brow. "Meaning?"

"Putrid," Holly said. "Well, you don't have to worry, Tutu. Tonoa is a very good cook, too. Interestingly enough, the two of you have something else in common. You both speak a lot of pidgin. You should get along famously.''

Tutu muttered something in Hawaiian, but Holly wasn't listening, for at that same moment, she realized Stump wasn't alone. A tall, willowy blond woman was standing beside him, wearing a peach-colored *holomu'u*, and carrying an assortment of leis over her arm.

Moments later, they were on the dock being introduced to Anita Miller, who put the white plumeria and pink carnation leis around their necks, huskily cooed an aloha greeting, and then wrapped an arm around Stump's waist while batting her inch-long eyelashes at him.

Stump flushed, and said, ''Ah, well, Anita and I go back a long way. Umm, actually, we were married back in the summer of '72. I was in the Merchant Marines then, and was land-locked in San Francisco while nursing a broken arm. Anita was a waitress in a little restaurant around the corner from the hotel where I was staying, and I knew I was in love the minute she offered to cut up my steak. Uh, well, you can imagine how surprised I was when she walked into the bar. She hasn't changed. No siree. Still as beautiful as ever, and still looks just like Betty Grable.''

Logan spoke up. "Maybe we should make arrangements to stay at one of the hotels, Stump. What with the renovation going on, and your unexpected company . . ."

Stump hit his peg leg on the dock with a resounding *thump.* "Wouldn't hear of it, mate. We've finished with the rooms upstairs, so about the only inconvenience you'll have is a bit of hammering now and then while we finish up the new shelves in the kitchen. I've had a few grumbling customers, but most of them have taken it in stride. They know it won't last forever."

"Then you didn't close the bar for the renovations?" Logan asked.

"Nope. I let everybody know ahead of time what I was going to do, and most of them voted to keep the place open. Said they would rather have a little sawdust in their drinks than have to go someplace else."

Anita was studying Logan through her long, sweeping lashes. And when she spoke, there was a cutting edge to her voice. "I was expecting somebody much older, Mr. West . . . Logan. Stump told me you're a retired cop."

Stump chuckled. "Guess I didn't make it all that clear. Logan had to retire after somebody knifed him in the back, but he still manages to stay in the thick of things, especially when it comes to law enforcement.''

Logan winked at Holly. ''It's the only way I can keep up with my wife.''

Anita lifted one elegantly tapered brow in Holly's direction. ''You're a cop, too?''

Wondering where in the lineup of Stump's four wives this woman belonged, and why Stump hadn't mentioned her when Logan called to tell him about their plans, Holly shook her head. ''I'm a private investigator.''

Stump returned, ''She's being modest, honeybunch. This pretty lady with the golden-red hair and sea-green eyes co-owns the St. James Detective Agency with her brother, Jack. Their pappy owned it, and they inherited it when he died.''

Anita didn't seem impressed. ''Oh, really. Stump said you live on Kauai, so I assume that's where you have the detective agency?''

Holly replied, ''It is.'' She exchanged glances with Logan, and could see the amusement in his eyes. *Honeybunch?*

Anita looked at Cindy and Danny. ''And I suppose the two of you are cops, too?''

''I'm in charge of security at one of the hotels,'' Danny said, ''and Cindy owns a gift shop in Lihue.''

Tutu puffed out her chest. ''And I take care of the house and important matters for *nani* Holly and *kane* Logan.''

''But Tutu is much more than a house-keeper,'' Logan said fondly. ''She's our island miracle, and is like a member of the family. We'd just about given up finding a suitable housekeeper when Tutu applied for the job, and it was love at first sight.''

''It must be something trying to keep house for these two, huh?'' Stump said, giving Tutu a lopsided grin.

Tutu returned his smile, and lifted her chin proudly. ''*Nani* house with much love. Tutu is happy, yeah. Garans.''

Stump threw back his head and laughed. ''You sound like Tonoa. Well, *I* guarantee you're gonna have a great time. We'd better go. By the time you have some refreshments and get settled in your rooms, Tonoa will have your dinner ready, and I can tell you right now, he's cooking up a feast.'' He looked down at the two suitcases. ''This can't be all of it. The last time you were here, Holly alone had no less than four.''

"This time, we decided to travel light," Logan said. "And Tutu has everything she needs in her satchel."

Danny spoke up. "You don't have to worry about a room for us, Stump. We're going to sleep on the *Sea Breeze.* We were married a couple of weeks ago, and we still haven't been able to find the time to take a honeymoon, so this is going to have to be it for a while."

"Ah, newlyweds!" Stump exclaimed. "I should've known by all the mushy stuff going on. These two"—he pointed at Holly and Logan—"still act like they are on *their* honeymoon, and it's been a whole year. Hard to believe it's been that long."

Holly dimpled up at Stump. "Does that mean you're going to give us the same room we had when we were here on our honeymoon? That wonderful room with the balcony?"

Stump cleared his throat. "Ahem . . ."

Anita raised her chin, almost defiantly. "*I'm* staying in the room with the balcony, but I really don't know why. The bed is lumpy, and I'd much rather have a view of the harbor than those ghastly mountains. But I *am* settled in, and moving can be such a bore."

"I wouldn't think of asking you to move, honeybunch," Stump said, giving Anita a hug. He looked at Holly and Logan imploringly. "Hope the two of you understand. Anita has been staying in that room nearly a month now, and has it all fixed up like home. You can take the room with the view of the harbor, and Tutu can have the room at the head of the stairs. That will leave one room vacant, so if you two lovebirds change your minds, just say so."

Danny said, "We won't change our minds. Do you live above the bar, too?"

Stump shook his head. "Nope. I was renting a little house across the alley in back, but the town decided to tear it down and turn the property into a park."

Holly wailed, "Oh, Stump! Your adorable little house!"

He shrugged. "Times change, things change. I'm renting a house a couple of blocks away now, and actually, I can't complain, because I have more room for my clutter."

Feeling a little disgruntled because Stump had been uprooted, and because she didn't remember the bed being lumpy at all, and because Anita's hateful opinion of the beautiful West Maui mountains was like a slap in the

face, Holly waited until they'd reached the bar
and were climbing the steps to the veranda before she said, "Why do you find the mountains
ghastly, Anita?"

Anita tossed over her shoulder, "They are
always shrouded in fog, for one thing, and it's
depressing. This is supposed to be sunny Hawaii, after all. If I wanted to see fog, I could
have gone to San Francisco."

Stump had opened the door, and Holly was
saved from what she *really* wanted to say—
Then why didn't you go to San Francisco?—
because they had literally stepped into a
pseudo tropical paradise. Dark green Astroturf
now covered the plank floor, woven baskets
filled with artificial flowers were stuffed everywhere, and polished cane and glass tables had
replaced the old wooden relics. The ceiling fan
was new and no longer creaked, the bartender
was now a tall, blond man with a sullen face,
and, worse, even the local patrons looked stiff
and uncomfortable. The wonderful island am-
bience, the atmosphere that had made Stump
Tanner's bar and eatery special, was gone.

Holly felt a lump form in her throat, noted
Stump had replaced the photo of Hedy Lamarr
above the bar with a photo of Betty Grable,

and asked, "Who was your decorator, Stump?"

"I was," Anita replied brightly. "And I couldn't believe the timing. The very day I arrived, Stump was pulling his hair out, trying to decide how to redecorate. Oh, he had all the basics covered, structurally speaking, and I probably wouldn't have said anything if he hadn't decided it would be simpler to leave the decor the way it was. That was when I stepped in, and made him realize just how shabby everything really looked. Tourists want to see a tropical paradise when they come to a place like this, *not* something out of a grade Z movie. You know, those horrid flicks depicting smoke-filled South Seas bars full of rowdy sailors and flirtatious island maidens. Class, that's the answer to success. Isn't that right, sugar cakes?"

Sugar cakes? Holly groaned inwardly, and was trying to think of a proper reprisal, when Tutu mumbled under her breath, "*Auwe! Malihini lolo.* Big *pilikia.*"

Holly heard the comment, and translated silently, *"Woe is me! The newcomer to the island is crazy. Big trouble."* Tutu had never been in the bar, and yet she had picked up on how bad it really looked. And as far as it having class, it had had class before, because it was real. Now, it was just a cheap imitation of something it was never meant to be.

Logan cleared his throat. "It sure looks different, Stump."

Stump nodded. "I know, and I'll admit there are times when I miss the way it was before, but Anita always did have a knack for making things pretty, and I'm all for making her happy."

At that moment, a crash sounded in the kitchen, and Stump rolled his eyes. "Either Tonoa dropped something, or he's throwing things again. You might as well sit down and relax. I'll be back as soon as I can get him settled down. Oh, and if you want something to drink, it's on the house."

Anita suggested the table in the corner because it would give them the best view of the harbor, and after they were seated, she lifted her chin pertly. "Stump wants to hire a waitress, but I've simply put my foot down. Good help is *so* hard to find, and why does he need a waitress when he has me?"

Logan looked up at her and smiled, though

it didn't reach his eyes. "Then I assume you're going to take our order?"

"I'll take your order. Just take it easy on the alcohol. It's better left to the paying customers, don't you think?"

Holly muttered, "Then we'll have five glasses of lemonade, with lots of ice, if you can spare it."

After Anita flounced off, Logan let out his breath in one big *swoosh*. "Whoa, what do you make of that?"

Holly gritted her teeth until her jaw ached. "I'd say she's after Stump again, and has already claimed the bar as her own. Let's hope she wasn't wife number four."

Cindy said a little wistfully, "I hate to say it, but she really is quite lovely."

Logan made a face. "She might be lovely, but her eyes are as hard as ice. I wonder if she knew Stump was on Maui, or if the meeting was by chance?"

"I have the feeling Anita Miller doesn't do anything 'by chance,'" Holly said, watching Stump stride across the floor, emphasizing every other step with his wooden leg. He looked like a man with a purpose, and his blue eyes were dark with anger.

He pulled up a chair from a nearby table, straddled it, and grumbled, "Maybe Anita is right. Maybe I should hire Ric, and toss Tonoa out with the dishwater."

"Ric?" Holly queried.

"Yeah. A guy from the mainland who's looking for a job as a cook. He claims he's as good as Wolfgang Puck. Anita thinks he'd be perfect, but I've been dragging my feet. Tonoa and I go back a long way. He was my cook when I opened up, and although his mood swings took some getting used to, I knew he was the best. Heck, he still is, but lately, he's been like a bear with its paw caught in a steel trap."

"Lately? Since when?" Holly asked.

"I dunno. The last few weeks, I guess."

Holly exchanged glances with Logan as Tutu said, "Tonoa is a Samoan name. Samoans have minds of their own."

Logan said, "So, did he drop something in the kitchen?"

"He says he did, but I think he was throwing things around. He's having trouble with the *haupia*. It won't set."

"Isn't *haupia* some kind of a pudding?" Danny asked.

"It's a light, gelatin-like dessert made from coconut," Logan replied.

Tutu stood up and announced, "Tutu makes a good *haupia*. I'll help Tonoa."

Stump frowned. "I don't know, Tutu. The kitchen is Tonoa's *kuleana*. His department."

But Tutu wasn't about to be dissuaded. After she marched off to the kitchen, Stump sighed. "She's as stubborn as he is."

"And she usually gets her way," Holly said, looking over at the bar. Anita was talking to the bartender, which brought another question to mind. "What happened to the other bartender, Stump? You know, the pretty lady who looked like Hedy Lamarr."

Stump shrugged. "I dunno. One day she was here, and the next day she was gone. Didn't even give me notice. Shortly after that, Brent walked in, looking for a job, and I hired him on the spot. He isn't pretty, and doesn't flirt with the customers, but he mixes a good drink. At least I haven't had any complaints."

"When was this?" Holly asked.

"Maybe two weeks ago. Isn't Anita something? She's my guest, and yet she insists on helping out." Anita was making her way across the room, and he literally beamed.

"Look at the way she's carrying the tray. She hasn't lost her touch, and she's as pretty as a picture."

Pretty and conniving, Holly thought, as Anita placed the tall, etched glasses on the table, and gave Stump a fetching smile.

At that moment, laughter drifted out from the kitchen, and the sound brought a smile to Holly's face. "Well, now, it looks as though Tutu and Tonoa are getting along famously. I thought they might."

"Tutu is in the kitchen with that . . . that cretin?" Anita asked incredulously.

Holly replied easily, "Yes, she certainly is, and I'll just bet you anything she'll end up turning the lion into a lamb." Holly took a sip of lemonade, forced it down, and said, "You're about to get your first complaint, Stump. The lemonade is terrible!"

Stump tasted it, and made a face. "Tastes like dishwater with a squirt of lemon-scented soap. If you'll excuse me, I think I'd better have a talk with my bartender."

"I'll do it," Anita said, walking across the room like a woman determined to tell the bartender off. But everybody at the table, except Stump, knew better. It had been *her* idea to serve them watered-down drinks, and the question was, why? It was only one of the many questions swirling around in Holly's head, and it left her with an old, familiar feeling she didn't like at all. Something was very, very wrong, and there was simply no way she was going to ignore it.

"Did Anita tell you how she happened to end up on Maui?" Holly asked Stump casually.

A smile replaced the scowl on his face. "Yeah, she did. She was vacationing on Lanai, and heard somebody mention Stump Tanner's bar in Lahaina. How's that for fate?"

"And you're okay with it?" Logan asked. "I mean, she *is* one of your ex-wives?"

"And she was the best of the four," Stump said proudly. "We were only married for a couple of months, the length of time it took for my arm to heal, but it left me with some pretty good memories." He looked around the table. "Uh-huh, I know what you're thinking. You're wondering why we split up after only a couple of months. I guess you'd have to understand what my life was like back in those days. I kept telling myself it was time to settle down, but I never could do it. The call of the sea was too strong, and I was always looking for the next adventure.

"Every time I fell in love, I kept hoping things would change, but they never did. Anita was the only wife who understood, and let me go without making a fuss. She got the divorce while I was out at sea, and I never saw her again. Well, until now."

"Then she didn't ask for alimony?" Logan asked.

"Naw. She knew I was broke."

"Did she know you were broke when she married you?"

"I wasn't broke when I married her, but by the time I left, most of it was gone." He gave a cryptic little sigh. "I spent it all on her, and to this day, I've never regretted it."

Logan said, "You told me your last wife wiped you out financially, and that was when you decided to become a confirmed bachelor. Were you talking about Anita? Was she the one who took all your money?"

"No way. Anita was my second wife. Eva was my fourth. By the time I married Eva, some ten years later, I'd managed to save up quite a bit of money. Maybe not as much as I had when I was married to Anita, but it was enough to hurt when I lost it, all the way to the bottom of my wallet.''

Logan pursued the questioning, and it was easy to see he didn't understand it, either. ''How much money are we talking about, Stump?''

Stump shrugged. ''I probably went through twenty grand with Anita, and Eva got me for ten.''

''Ten grand?'' When Stump nodded, Logan pressed on. ''So, you spent twenty grand on Anita in two months' time, and handed ten grand over to Eva when you were divorced. Frankly, my friend, I don't see much difference.''

Stump's eyes twinkled. ''Ah, but that's where you're wrong. I enjoyed spending money on Anita because we were able to share in the good times together.''

Danny offered, ''Must have been pretty good times to go through twenty grand in two months.''

''They were the best,'' Stump returned. ''Short, but oh, so sweet.

''Now, if you'll excuse me, I'd better check on things in the kitchen. It's pretty quiet, so let's hope Tonoa hasn't stuffed Tutu in the freezer.''

After he'd gone, Logan scowled, and lowered his voice. "Something isn't sitting well, Holly. Call it a gut feeling, if you want, but I think Stump is about to walk off the plank again, without even realizing it.''

Holly looked at Logan and sighed. ''That's why we work so well together, my handsome husband. We think alike. Anita didn't just pop up unexpectedly. She's here to take Stump for every cent he has, again, and this time, if you add in the bar, he has a lot more than twenty thousand stashed away for a rainy day.''

Cindy looked at Danny helplessly. ''I have the feeling this romantic island venture is about to take on new dimensions, and that's what we get for being friends with a couple of crime busters.''

Logan grinned. "If that's anything like 'Ghostbusters,' we're flattered. Seriously, if Stump is in trouble, you can't expect us to look the other way. But for now, we'll let it rest. We still have Tonoa's feast to look forward to. . . .''

''As well as the sunset and the soft island evening,'' Holly added, kissing Logan's cheek.

"Shall we take our luggage upstairs and freshen up?"

Cindy rested her head against Danny's shoulder. "Don't let them fool you. They want to go upstairs so they can talk about the new 'case' that just happened to drop at their feet."

"Well, at least it isn't a murder case," Logan teased, taking Holly's hand. "Ready, my love?"

"Ready," Holly said, silently listing the questions she wanted to ask him and hoped he could answer.

Chapter Two

Stump insisted on setting up a special table on the veranda for the foursome, remembering how much Holly and Logan had enjoyed dining there. They were afforded a spectacular view, and a sunset that simply defied description in its ethereal beauty. The veranda also provided a certain amount of privacy from the evening crowd, but they weren't so far away they couldn't hear the soft, romantic strains of the Hawaiian combo, or the laughter and camaraderie inside, as the locals and tourists bid aloha to another island day.

Only Anita seemed miffed by the arrangement, claiming she couldn't *possibly* serve the customers properly inside, *and* keep running out to the veranda.

Stump was in the middle of reminding her of the fact that he waited tables, too, and would be more than happy to take care of his friends, when Tutu announced she was taking over, and the subject was closed. She had already eaten in the kitchen, while helping Tonoa prepare the feast, so the table was only set for four, and oh, what a setting it was! Stump had brought out his personal dishes—heavy, earthenware pieces he'd purchased in Zanzibar—and a basket heaped with *real* flowers (Tutu's idea, knowing how much Holly hated artificial flowers) had been placed in the center of the table, and the sweet scent of them was wonderful as candles flickered in the gentle breeze, and garlands of colorful lanterns danced overhead.

The foursome had dressed for the occasion, too, with the men in white pants and colorful aloha shirts, and although Cindy had decided to wear slacks and a blouse, while Holly wore a sweeping muumuu, both *wahines* had put a spray of vanda orchids in their hair.

It was a night meant for lovers, and probably would have been if, after Tutu served the first course of delightful crabmeat soup with wild

Haiku mushrooms, Cindy hadn't said, "Okay, you two. This is all *really* lovely, and I'm *really* hungry, but I'm not going to be able to eat a bite if you don't bring us up to date."

Holly grinned at Logan. "You hear that, honey? We were upstairs for only an hour, and yet she's making it sound as though we were gone a week, and during that time we were able to obtain a whole dossier on one Anita Miller."

Cindy tossed her head. "Well, don't you? I mean, don't you have a dossier on Anita Miller? An hour can be a long time if its used wisely."

Danny swallowed a mouthful of soup, and sighed. "You'd better listen to her. She's talking from experience. We had one hour to freshen up and get ready, too, and believe me, she used it to her advantage. By the time we left the *Sea Breeze*, she had all the questions she put to me, and I couldn't answer, in absolute order so she could lay them out for you."

Cindy shrugged. "That's what happens when you're best friends with a P.I. and a cop. So, did you come to the conclusion that history is going to repeat itself? I mean, do you really think Anita is here to do a number on Stump's finances, and if so, what are you planning to do about it?''

"Nothing for now," Logan said easily.

"Because sometimes, it's simply better to sit back, observe, and listen," Holly added. "Facts solve cases, not speculation. Besides, it's easy to see that Stump is really smitten with the lady, and we'd never be able to convince him she's up to no good without solid proof."

"So, how are you going to get the proof?" Cindy asked. She rolled her eyes. "I know. You're going to sit back, observe, and listen."

"That's right," Holly said. "I have a long list of questions, too, Cindy, and hopefully somewhere along the line, we'll find the answers. First of all, Stump told us Anita was vacationing on Lanai when she heard somebody mention Stump Tanner's bar in Lahaina. Well, I don't know how familiar you guys are with Lanai, but it's like an island time forgot, and doesn't even remotely resemble the kind of place that would appeal to a woman like Anita Miller."

"The 'Pineapple Island,' " Danny announced cheerfully. "Established by John Dole in 1922. Now, the Doles' Hawaiian Pineapple Company and the parent company, Castle and Cooke, are trying to turn the little island into a place that will attract tourists. But as I understand it, it's slow going. When I decided to move from the mainland five years ago, I studied up on all the islands, trying to decide which one would be best suited for me. Lanai sounded like a terrific spot for somebody who wanted remote and rustic, and wasn't looking for a job in hotel security. I think they only had one hotel at the time, and it wasn't very big.''

Holly replied, ''Exactly, and even now, they only have two, not counting the old hotel in Lanai City. I think Anita found out Stump was here some other way, and this was a setup from the beginning.''

Logan said with a grin, ''We've decided the best place to start sleuthing is on Lanai. We'll take the *Sea Breeze* over tomorrow.''

''Tutu's son and his family live on Lanai, so that will give us a legitimate reason to be there,'' Holly offered. ''We'd love to have you join us, and of course we'll take Tutu. . . .''

''Tutu not go to Lanai except on a plane,'' Tutu announced, catching the last of the conversation as she padded across the veranda. "Tutu not go on *any* boat until time to go home. I visit *keiki* last week on days off, and visit was meant to last a month. You say aloha, and aloha for me, and *ohana* will understand." Her dark eyes narrowed over the bowls of soup, and she clucked her tongue. "Nobody eat except *kane* Danny. *Kaukau* is bad?"

Holly gave Tutu an appreciative smile. "The food is wonderful, Tutu. We've just been busy talking, that's all. Give us another few minutes, and you can serve the next course."

Moments later, Stump thumped across the veranda, carrying a bottle of champagne and four glasses. He gave them an apologetic shrug, and sighed. "Should have brought this out to you a lot sooner, but I got into a little tiff with Anita."

Holly said, "Let me guess. She thought you should save the champagne for the paying customers."

"Well, yeah, but I understand, even if I don't agree. She has my best interests at heart." He finally smiled. "But, hey, it's not every day of the week I get to cater to my good friends. You want another bottle later on, let me know."

After Tutu and Stump had gone inside,
Holly shook her head. "Well, at least he got
his way, and that's encouraging." She eyed
Cindy intently. "So, do you guys have any
plans for tomorrow?"

"I'd love to do some sleuthing," Cindy admitted, "but Danny wants to explore Lahaina."

Danny teased, "If you really want to
'sleuth,' honeybunch, we can save Lahaina for
another day."

Cindy returned, "Just for that, *sugar cakes*,
I ought to leave you in Lahaina all by yourself
for a month." She squeezed Danny's hand, and
smiled at Holly. "I'll leave the detective work
to you two, and spend the day with my handsome husband. And who knows, maybe we'll
uncover something here."

Danny groaned. "Does that sound like she
plans to leave the detective work to you?"

Cindy had finished her soup, and dabbed at
her mouth with a napkin. "You said something
earlier, Holly, and I just have to ask. You were
talking about Lanai, and how you didn't think
it would appeal to a woman like Anita Miller.
Care to elaborate? A woman like what?"

Holly replied, "Well, she's very cosmopolitan, for one thing. She might be wearing island apparel and I think she has gone to great lengths to fit in, but I can see the loathing in her eyes. She abhors everything about island life.''

"Especially the West Maui Mountains," Logan added. ''It also occurred to us she was probably responsible for getting rid of the pretty female bartender who looked like Hedy Lamarr. Stump said she left without giving notice, so how much do you want to bet the two faced off in a confrontation, and Anita won?''

"No bet," Cindy said. "Anita probably saw her as competition.''

Danny said thoughtfully, "Well, there is no way she can see Tonoa as competition, so why does she want to get rid of him?''

Logan spoke up. ''I think Tonoa sees her for what she is, and she knows it. Maybe she's afraid he will eventually convince Stump, and she'll be the one who ends up getting tossed out on her ear.''

"Well, let's keep that lovely thought," Holly said, smiling at Tutu as she carried the salad tray to the table. ''Did you really eat, Tutu? Or did you just grab a bite here and there?''

Tutu placed the salad plates filled with lettuce and tiny bay shrimp on the table, and her dark eyes danced. ''Tutu and Tonoa grabbed a bit here and there. Kitchen closes at eleven. Eat much *kaukau* then. Then go *holoholo*, yeah.''

After Tutu padded off, humming a little tune, Logan chuckled. ''If you didn't get all that, she said that after the kitchen closes at eleven, they are going to eat a lot of food, and then go for a walk. I'd say we have the beginning of a blossoming romance.''

''Well, this is certainly the place for it,'' Holly said dreamily, looking out at the sunset that had turned the sky a deep russet color tinged with orange and pink.

Logan kissed Holly's cheek. ''Then I suggest we stick to romance, and leave the sleuthing for tomorrow.''

It was easy to agree, especially when the main course was succulent, honey-dipped chicken, and along with the creamy *haupia* for dessert, they were served thick slabs of pineapple cheesecake and cups of rich Kona coffee. Especially when after dinner, Logan suggested a walk in the moonlight. It was all wonderfully romantic, and Holly gave in to the moment, and could almost forget their dear friend was in trouble. Almost, but not quite, though it was Logan who finally brought it up, for it had been preying on his mind, too.

"Going to Lanai might be a waste of time, Holly. Anita has been in Lahaina for a month, and with so much tourist traffic, people have a tendency to forget faces."

"But Lanai doesn't get the normal tourist traffic, and she really is quite striking. Besides, she looks like Betty Grable."

"Yeah, but unless we run into a movie buff or somebody from that era, we'll more than likely get, 'Betty who?' "

"Then you don't think we should go?"

They had reached the alley behind the bar, and Logan shrugged. "Guess it wouldn't hurt to think of it as a little side trip for our own pleasure. I'd suggest going in the bar the back way, but it's after eleven, and if Tutu and Tonoa are having a romantic dinner—" He broke off, and pulled Holly back, so they were standing in shadows instead of moonlight. And with his mouth close to her ear, he whispered, "Take a look down at the end of the alley. Blond hair and a pink *holomu'u*."

The alley wasn't long, and the bar was the last establishment before the alley jutted into a tangle of vines and foliage. It was Anita, and she wasn't alone. "Isn't that the bartender?" Holly whispered, noting the way they were huddled together.

"It sure is," Logan returned. "We'd better backtrack around the block, and go in the front."

"What are you going to say to Stump?" Holly asked, hurrying to keep up with Logan's long strides.

"I don't know. Maybe nothing. Maybe it's all perfectly innocent, and they're just taking a break."

"You don't believe that any more than I do, and there is something else. Did you see the addition to the balcony?"

"I saw it. Stairs leading down to the alley. I wonder whose idea that was?"

Questions were piling up again, and Holly felt the first tug of real apprehension. The female bartender had left under suspicious circumstances, and now the bartender was a stranger named Brent. A tall, moody man with blond hair who, now that she thought about it, looked enough like Betty Grable to be her brother. . . .

* * *

There were only a few customers in the bar, and the island combo was wrapping it up for the night. Stump was behind the bar polishing glasses, and grinned when Holly and Logan walked in. "Nothing like taking a romantic walk in the moonlight. How about a cup of coffee?"

"Sounds great," Holly said, sliding up on a barstool. "Is Tutu still in the kitchen?"

"Naw. She took off with Tonoa. The last I heard, they were going to his brother's house, so she can meet the family. They sure hit it off. I haven't seen a smile on Tonoa's face like that since his sister had twins."

"So, where is your bartender?" Logan asked, taking a seat beside Holly.

"Business is slow, so I gave him the rest of the night off."

"And Anita?" Holly asked casually.

"She's upstairs with a migraine headache."

After Stump poured coffee into two mugs, Holly cleared her throat. "We were walking around in back, and noticed you've put in stairs leading from the balcony to the alley."

Stump nodded. "That was Anita's idea."

"So, you just recently made the addition?"

"Finished it a week ago. She wanted to be

able to come and go without having to walk through the bar. Especially at night, after everything is closed up.''

''Does she usually 'come and go' late at night?'' Holly asked.

''Only when she can't sleep. I'm afraid she's a bit of an insomniac. Did you see the park?''

Logan spoke up. ''Well, yes and no. It was pretty dark. We'll get a better look at it tomorrow.''

Stump sighed. ''I miss the little house, but my sentimentality can't get in the way of progress. We've had a lot of changes in town, and I've heard it's only the beginning.''

''Progress can be a good thing for the economy,'' Logan said gently. ''And I would think having a park close to your bar would be good for business. Tourists will undoubtedly see the park as a good place to rest, and the bar as the place to get a tall, cool drink. Maybe you should put a sign in the back of the building so it can be seen from the park. Maybe even list a few specials now and then. You know, iced tea, fifty cents a glass or a bottle of beer for a buck.''

Stump seemed pleased with the idea, and said, ''Just might do that. More coffee?''

Holly shook her head. "I'm going to turn in. It's been a long day. Logan?"

Logan gave her a hug. "You go ahead, sweetheart. I'd like to talk to Stump for a few minutes, but I won't be long."

Holly nodded, and climbed the stairs, but her thoughts were on Anita, who was in the alley having a clandestine meeting with the bartender, when she was supposed to be in her room, nursing a migraine headache. She'd lied to Stump, and now all Holly had to do was figure out why.

Chapter Three

Holly was on her fourth cup of coffee the following morning when Logan joined her on the veranda, pointed at the untouched pineapple coffeecake on the table, and admonished, "You'd better eat some of that to counteract all the caffeine you've consumed, sweetheart, or your nerves are going to be jangling like wind chimes in the breeze."

Holly raised her face for his sweet kiss, and sighed. "And how do you know how much coffee I've consumed?"

"Tutu told me. She's also concerned because you didn't sleep well, but then I already knew that. You tossed and turned half the night, and I saw you slip out of the room around five.''

"I didn't mean to disturb you," she said, taking his hand.

He kissed her fingers, and returned, "You didn't. I didn't sleep well, either. We just approach it differently, that's all I lie there with my eyes closed and think, while you do a lot of pillow punching. Can't say my way is any better than yours, because I'm just as perplexed now as I was when I went to bed. I stayed down in the bar last night so I could have a heart-to-heart with Stump, and all I ended up doing was lending an ear, so he could tell me how delighted he is to have Anita back in his life.''

Holly gave Logan an apologetic smile. "And I meant to stay awake so we could discuss Stump's perplexing problem, but the bed felt so good, and I was so tired. Unfortunately, I only slept a couple of hours before I had a bad dream, and I couldn't go back to sleep from that point on. I don't remember the dream, exactly, but I know it was about Anita, and it was unsettling.''

Logan poured a cup of coffee, and looked at

his watch. "Speaking of Anita, don't suppose you've seen her this morning?"

"No, I haven't, but I'll admit I was surprised to see Tutu up so bright and early. It was very late when she got in last night, and yet there she is, in the kitchen baking bread, and singing at the top of her lungs. She said she wants to surprise Tonoa when he comes in at nine, and I told her that with all those wonderful smells wafting around, she'll have tourists coming out of the woodwork, thinking the bar serves breakfast."

"That's exactly what I'm going to tell her," Stump said, climbing the side steps to the veranda. "I could smell the bread a block away. Anita thinks I should start serving breakfast, but that would mean I'd have to get to the bar before daybreak every morning, and that's too early for me. Things suit me fine just the way they are. I get up at seven, get to the bar around eight, Tonoa arrives around nine, and we open at ten-thirty for the early lunch crowd."

"But it isn't even seven," Holly reasoned. "I hope you didn't get up early because of us."

Stump ran a hand through his spiky white hair, and frowned. "To tell you the truth, I hardly slept at all last night. I kept worrying about Anita. That's the second migraine head-ache she's had in a week. Have you seen her this morning?''

Holly replied quickly, ''She hasn't come down yet, Stump, but that might be for the best. You said she's a bit of an insomniac, so maybe a good night's sleep is exactly what she needs.''

Stump shrugged. ''Maybe.'' He eyed the coffee cake. ''Did Tutu bake that?''

Logan grinned. ''Yeah, she did, and there are two more cooling on the counter. She also has a couple of chickens simmering on the stove so she can make her knockout chicken salad for the lunch crowd, and she was talking about making Tonoa's favorite chocolate torte.''

Stump shook his head. ''Tonoa has been try-ing to make that particular dessert for a couple of years, and it flops every time.''

Logan winked at Holly. ''We told you she's a gem in the kitchen.''

Stump's blue eyes twinkled. ''I have the feeling Tonoa thinks she's a gem, too, in more ways than one.''

After Stump went inside, Holly shook her

head. "I had to bite my tongue to keep from telling him about Anita and the bartender."

"I know, and it's a sad state of affairs. I've been thinking. Maybe we should get Anita aside, and talk to her."

"Maybe . . ." Holly looked over Logan's shoulder, and frowned. Cindy and Danny were hurrying across the street with a tall, lanky man wearing tan chino pants and an aloha shirt, and she would have recognized him anywhere. It was Homicide Detective Al Gainer.

Logan caught Holly's surprised expression, turned around, and groaned. "Boy oh boy, I don't like the looks of that."

Holly didn't like it, either, and by the time the threesome reached the veranda, she found herself holding her breath. Cindy looked very pale and shaken, and Danny didn't look much better.

Danny held Cindy close and muttered, "I know this is going to be hard to believe, but we . . . We decided to go for a walk this morning, and . . ."

Cindy's chin trembled. "We wanted to get an early start because it was such a glorious morning. We were walking along the wharf, watching the first rays of light. . . . I-I saw the tarp first. I thought it was some sort of a package, until . . .'' Tears filled her eyes, and she looked away.

Al Gainer gave Holly a hug, shook Logan's hand, and then motioned to Cindy and Danny. ''You two sit down, and take a couple of deep breaths. I'll do the talking.'' He nodded toward the bar, and lowered his voice. ''Is Stump around?''

Holly murmured, ''He's inside.''

''Anybody else?''

''Just Tutu, our housekeeper. She and Tonoa are getting along famously, and she's baking bread and doing all sorts of things in the kitchen to surprise him when he comes in at nine.''

''Okay, then I'll talk low and fast. Danny, here, called headquarters around five, to report a dead body.''

Holly sucked in her breath. ''Oh, no!''

Al sighed. ''I know. Great way to start a honeymoon, huh? I have to tell you, when I found out they are on a honeymoon of sorts, and came over from Kauai with you guys to help you celebrate your anniversary, I got a royal case of déjà vu, remembering another honeymoon a year ago, when you had a dead body all but drop at your feet.

"Anyway, it just so happens I was in my office when Danny called. I was behind in the paperwork, and decided to get an early start. So much for the paperwork."

Danny spoke up. "We both thought it was some sort of a package, until we saw the hand."

Feeling a little light-headed, Holly choked out, "Where did you find it?"

"Floating in the water near the wharf," Al said. "The killer used a painter's drop cloth and a length of rope to wrap up the body. We'll have to wait until the autopsy to confirm this, but from all preliminary indications, it was a shooting, and the killer knew what he was doing. One bullet through the heart. Quick and clean."

Cindy had picked up a napkin off the table, and was twisting it around in her hands. "It gets worse," she said, closing her eyes against the pain of remembering.

Danny bit at his bottom lip, and sighed. "We . . . We were there when the cops unwrapped the body. When I saw the pink *holomu'u*, I knew it was a woman, and then . . ."

Holly's heart nearly stopped, and she couldn't help but gasp. "Anita Miller?"

Al grimaced before he replied, "She wasn't carrying identification, but Cindy and Danny recognized her, and gave us a statement. Stump will still have to identify the body, as well as answer some questions, and I have to tell you, it's days like this that make me wish I'd taken up chicken ranching."

"Stump is going to be devastated," Logan said sadly.

Holly grasped Logan's hand. "Maybe we could have prevented it, Logan. If we'd come clean with Stump last night . . ."

When Al raised a brow, Logan explained. "Holly and I took a walk last night, and saw Anita and Stump's new bartender in the alley."

"I heard he had a new male bartender. Tall and blond, right? So, were they arguing? Talking? Or what?"

"They were at the far end so it was difficult to tell, but they looked pretty chummy."

"Did they see you?"

"No. We backtracked, and went in the front way. That was when Stump told us Anita had a migraine headache, and had gone up for the night."

Al frowned. "And he didn't see her come back downstairs?"

Holly explained about the balcony steps leading to the alley, and added, "Stump said she was an insomniac, and was accustomed to taking late-night walks, which was apparently the reason for putting in the stairs. Her idea, not his. It's really bizarre, Al, because we had hardly gotten off the *Sea Breeze*, and we were questioning her motives for being here. Did Danny and Cindy tell you Stump was married to her a long time ago?"

Danny nodded. "We told him, along with some of the other stuff we discussed."

Al flipped open a notebook. "So far, I have three pages of unanswered questions. But first things first. I have to talk to Stump, and make arrangements to go through the victim's things. Maybe we'll find some answers there. Meanwhile, I want the four of you to put your heads together, and compile a list of everything you remember regarding one Anita Miller from the time you arrived in Lahaina, and that includes your impressions, no matter how insignificant."

Logan ran a hand through his dark, wavy hair. "Holly and I were going to sail over to

Lanai this morning, and do some poking around. Supposedly, Anita was vacationing there when she heard somebody mention Stump Tanner's bar in Lahaina. That's what brought her here. Stump calls it fate; Holly calls it a setup.''

Al's dark eyes narrowed in thought. ''Then poking around still might be a good idea.''

''I agree,'' Logan said, ''but it would be better if we had a photo. We'll wait until after you've gone through her things, on the off chance you find one.''

''Did you ask Stump if he has a photo?'' Al asked.

''No, because we didn't want him to know what we were up to. Now, I guess it doesn't matter.''

Al shoved the notebook in his pocket. ''What about the bartender. You know anything about him?''

Holly shook her head. ''Only that his name is Brent, he's the sullen type, and looks enough like Anita to be her brother.''

Logan added, ''About two weeks ago, Stump's bartender walked out unexpectedly. It wasn't long after that, Brent applied for the job, and got it.''

Al shook his head. "Bet that was a blow. Lila was a true island beauty, and the customers loved her. Any idea why she walked out?"

"Nothing conclusive," Holly replied, "but it did occur to us that Anita might have had something to do with it, if she thought of Lila as competition."

Al managed a smile. "That's the kind of stuff I want you to put down." He reached in a pocket, pulled out a microcassette recorder, and handed it to Logan. "No need to write it down. Just talk into this. I'll sort it out later."

After Al walked into the bar, Holly said, "Maybe you should go with him, Logan. Stump is going to need a friend."

"Before this is over, he's going to need *all* his friends," Logan returned, "but there isn't much I can do at the moment. It's going to take some time for him to absorb what's happened, and then try to deal with it."

For the next half hour, they took turns speaking into the recorder, and although Holly contributed, her thoughts were with Stump, and what a terrible nightmare he must be going through.

Finally, Logan clicked off the recorder, and

sighed. "It's sure quiet inside. Maybe I'd better check on things."

But it wasn't necessary, for at that moment, Stump plodded out on the veranda. He'd been crying, but offered them a wan smile. "Guess it's safe to say, there's never a dull minute at Stump Tanner's bar and eatery, in beautiful, downtown Lahaina." He sat down heavily, as though the weight of the world had been dumped on his shoulders. "Al told me you questioned Anita's motives for being here, right from the beginning. Well, I sure didn't see anything questionable, and now I feel like a fool."

"You were in love with her," Holly said gently, "and they say love is blind."

Stump took a deep, ragged breath. "I don't know if I was in love with her, exactly, but she sure was like a breath of fresh air."

"Where is Al?" Logan asked.

"Up in Anita's room with a couple of cops. They came in the back way. Thought that would be better than drawing attention to a cop car parked out front. Though I don't know. Now with that park across the alley, privacy is a thing of the past. Guess I should close up for a few days, but part of me is telling the other part to stay open, otherwise I'll have too much time on my hands to think, and worry. Bottom line, there is a cold-blooded killer out there, and that's one scary thought.''

Holly couldn't hold back the shiver. ''Does Tutu know what's happened?''

Stump rubbed a hand over his eyes. ''She knows. She came out of the kitchen just as Al was saying I would have to identify Anita's body. Al gave her a brief accounting, and after telling him he was lucky *nani* Holly and *kane* Logan were on the island to help him with the investigation, she hurried back to the kitchen and began chanting in Hawaiian. I'd say she's praying to some long-dead king or queen, or maybe even Madam Pele herself.''

''Prayers can't hurt,'' Holly said, giving Stump's arm a comforting squeeze.

''Do you think your bartender is involved?'' Danny asked.

Stump shrugged. ''Maybe. If nothing else, he was probably the last person to see her alive.'' His eyes narrowed over Logan. ''You should've told me, mate.''

Logan's sigh was heartfelt. ''I wanted to, Stump. That's why I stayed so late in the bar last night. But instead of telling you what we saw in the alley, I ended up listening to you list all the reasons why you were happy to have Anita back in your life.''

''Do you know where the bartender is staying?'' Holly asked.

Stump nodded. ''He has a room at the Pioneer Inn. Al made arrangements to have him picked up for questioning.'' He sighed again. ''Guess, at least for today, I'll have to wear two hats. Waiter and bartender.''

Holly spoke up quickly. ''Logan can go to Lanai alone. I'll stay here and wait tables, Stump.''

Cindy, who had finally composed herself, lifted her chin and announced, ''Danny can go to Lanai with Logan, and I'll stay here with you, Holly. Stump can use the extra help, and I don't mind waiting tables.''

Holly thought for a minute Stump was going to protest, but then his shoulders slumped in defeat. He knew better than to argue, and had just muttered, ''Thanks,'' when Al strode out onto the veranda, looking dark, rumpled, and angry.

''Uh-oh,'' Logan said. ''Don't tell me something else has happened.''

''You could say that,'' Al returned, tossing

a photograph on the table. "Turn it over, and read the back."

Logan turned it over, and Holly read along with him:

Hope you like this, sis. I think it's the best picture we've ever had taken together. At least we're both smiling, and you aren't squinting at the camera like you usually do. Love, Brent.

"So they were brother and sister," Holly said, handing the photo to Stump.

He glanced at it, and shook his head. "It occurred to me they looked a lot alike, but I never considered the possibility they might be brother and sister."

Al said, "Yeah, well, that, and the latest development, puts the whole thing in a different perspective. For starters, Brent 'Smith' isn't registered at the Pioneer Inn, and never was."

"Did you try Brent Miller?" Logan asked.

"I did, and got zilch there, too. I have my men checking out the other hotels, but I have to tell you, I have a bad feeling about this, because I find it pretty hard to believe he killed his sister. So, unless we can track him down,

or unless he shows up for work today, oblivi-
ous to what's happened, then I can only assume he's met foul play, too, and we have
another body out there, somewhere.''

It was a chilling thought, and fear squeezed
Holly's heart as she said, ''Maybe they were
running from somebody, and that somebody finally found them. It would explain all the se-
crecy, and why somebody like Anita was
vacationing on remote and rustic Lanai.''

Logan added, ''And then out of the blue, she
hears someone mention Stump Tanner's bar in
Lahaina. It's easy to see how she could have
thought of it as the perfect place to hide out.''

Holly asked, ''What about the name 'Miller,' Stump? Was that Anita's maiden name?''

Stump shook his head. ''She was married
again after she divorced me. That one lasted a
year. She kept his name because she thought it
sounded good with 'Anita.' Unless she was fib-
bing to me, and the name was an alias.''

Al muttered, ''Like 'Smith.' Are you ready
to roll, Stump? The coroner is waiting for us.''

Stump actually turned pale under his dark
tan, but nodded. ''As ready as I'll ever be.''

Al reached the steps before he said, ''I'm

leaving a man here in the event the brother shows up. He's dressed in civvies, so hopefully, he won't draw too much attention.''

Logan said, ''That sounds like he might draw attention no matter what he's wearing.''

Al grinned. ''You could say that. His name is Joe, but his nickname is Pupule Mauna. Means 'crazy mountain.' That's because he's six-feet-six, weighs three hundred pounds, and has the tendency to go ballistic now and again. But he's still one heck of a cop, and dependable, so you can rest easy, Logan. With Joe around, the ladies will be well protected.''

Al had forgotten the photo, and Logan held it up. ''What about the photo?''

''Take it to Lanai, and show it around. We can always make copies later. On that note, we're outta here.''

''And so are we,'' Logan said, kissing Holly's cheek. ''Hopefully, we won't be gone long. Promise me you'll be good and won't give Joe Pupule Mauna a bad time?''

Logan was trying to make light of it, but she could see the concern in his golden brown eyes. She wouldn't have expected less, because he loved her, and would be remiss if he wasn't worried. ''I'll be good if you'll be careful,'' she teased back, and then whispered, ''*Aloha au ia oe*, my darling. I love you forever and ever, and even after that.''

Chapter Four

Even though Al's description of Joe had given Holly a good idea of what to expect, the giant of a man still took her breath away when he lumbered down the stairs and into the bar area later that morning. Wearing tan-colored walking shorts, a bright-blue aloha shirt, and zoris on his oversized feet, he was a striking figure of a man. And oh, the smile! Wide and sparkling bright, and there was no denying the warmth in his dark brown eyes as he made his way toward Holly and Cindy, who were slicing lemons and limes at the bar.

Introductions were quickly made, and then he said, in a deep, resounding voice, "Al told me I was in for a treat. Said the two of you were the prettiest *wahines* on the island. Even prettier than an Olowalu sunrise. Well, he sure wasn't kidding.''

Cindy giggled. ''Oh, you're *so* sweet!''

Holly smiled up at him. ''Flattery will get you everywhere, Officer. . . .''

''It's Sergeant Joseph Kaloni, but my friends call me Joe.'' He held up a key. ''I've locked the room, and have the stairs to the alley cordoned off, so now I've got some time for a cup of coffee. I'd order lunch, but I guess it's a little early, and I sure don't want to throw things off in the kitchen.''

''You won't throw things off,'' Holly said. ''The last time I looked, everything was just about ready, with the exception of the baked *uku*.''

''Okay, then I'll just sit myself down at that corner table over there, and start with a large bowl of Tonoa's vegetable soup. After that, Tonoa knows the drill. Two cheeseburgers with everything, a double order of Maui onion rings, and a slice of pineapple cheesecake for dessert.''

Finally, with the bowl of vegetable soup in front of him, Joe smiled up at Holly as she was filling his water glass, and said, "Now, how about you, Holly St. James West? Will you join me? I know you and Cindy are helping Stump out, but the way I see it, everything seems to be under control, and even pretty *wahines* have to eat." He gave her a sheepish grin. "Okay, I can see by the expression on your face you're questioning my motives. Guess that shouldn't be a surprise. Al said you're a first-rate P.I. and if you managed to get me cornered, you'd probably bend my ear, both with questions and opinions. So, sit down, relax, and let's talk about the homicide."

"I thought you'd never ask," Holly teased. "But to be honest, I couldn't eat a bite, Joe. I'm full of nervous energy, and double that on anxiety. Doesn't do much to stimulate the appetite."

His dark eyes twinkled mischievously. "And that's why you keep your pretty figure. It's easy to see you're the type who runs on nervous energy. Just like my wife. And you're probably every bit as tenacious."

"I'll admit to being a bit tenacious, but right now, I'm also deeply concerned. Stump has been gone nearly three hours, and the police station is only a few blocks away. Should I be worried?''

Joe shrugged. ''Wouldn't take him long to identify the body, but the questioning might take forever. Knowing Al, he'll want Stump to give him every detail since Anita Miller's arrival on the island. No sign of the brother, huh?''

''Not yet, though he isn't scheduled to come in until noon. That's when the bar officially opens for drinks.''

''So, do you think he'll show?''

''No, I don't. He either knows what happened to his sister and is on the run, or he's dead, too.''

''Then you don't think he killed his sister?''

Holly sighed. ''I don't want to believe it, Joe. I suppose it's because I love my brother with all my heart, and he loves me, and I can't imagine something like that happening.''

''Yeah, well that's kinda the way I feel. I got me a brother, too, and although he can be a bit of a pain, I'd put my life down for him, and I know he'd do the same for me.''

''So, assuming Anita's brother is alive, did you find anything in her room that might help us locate him?''

After adding a handful of oyster crackers to the soup, Joe shook his head. "Didn't find any reference to the brother at all but for that one photo. Wouldn't have found that if Al hadn't looked through her books. He found it in the back of *Hawaii, Off the Beaten Path.*"

Holly returned, "Which supports my theory that Anita and her brother were running from somebody, and were looking for out-of-the-way places to hide. What did you find in her purse? She wasn't carrying identification when they found her body, so I assume she left her purse behind?"

"She did, but we didn't find much. Cosmetics, a bottle of pikake perfume, chewing gum, a key ring, and a paperback novel."

"Billfold?"

"Nope. And no identification of any kind, not even a credit card. She had close to a hundred bucks in an empty candy jar, and some loose change on a table."

"What was on the key ring?"

"Two keys, probably a house key and a car key, and a pink rabbit's foot. So much for the rabbit's foot bringing her good luck."

Joe had finished the soup, and was working his way through the first cheeseburger when

Cindy placed a bowl of soup in front of Holly, and announced, "Orders from the kitchen. You're supposed to eat every drop."

Grudgingly, Holly made an attempt, but her thoughts were on the room upstairs. Finally, she said, "Stump said Anita had the room 'fixed up like home,' so I assume that means it's full of her personal belongings?"

"Not really, unless you want to call an assortment of artificial flowers and island bric-a-brac personal. You know, the kind of stuff tourists buy up by the bagful to take home as souvenirs."

"Clothes?"

"A couple of muumuus and *holomu'us*, but mostly jeans and western shirts. Not exactly the kind of clothing you'd normally pack for an island vacation. One medium-size, empty suitcase, so I'd say she was traveling light.

"So, you and your brother own a detective agency on Kauai. Do you get much business?"

"Enough to keep the bills paid, but right now, things are slow. That's why I was able to take the time off. . . . Would it be possible for me to look at Anita's room?"

"I don't have a problem with that. We've done all we can, and the rest will be up to

Stump. You know, like packing up her things.'' He gave Holly the key, and a lopsided grin. ''Don't look now, but you finished the soup.''

Holly looked down at the empty bowl and shrugged. ''Guess I must have been hungrier than I thought, or my subconscious knows better than to oppose Tutu's orders.'' She explained about Tutu, and added, ''Tonoa is proof enough of her incredible influence. He's been smiling since our arrival.''

''I met her when I came in the back way,'' Joe offered, ''and from what I observed, I'd say he's in love.''

Holly sighed wistfully. ''Love can be wonderful, if you fall in love with the right person. If you don't, it can break your heart.''

''Are you thinking about Stump?''

Holly shook her head. ''No, not really. He all but admitted he wasn't really in love with Anita. I was just talking in generalities, and counting my own blessings because I have Logan.''

Joe said, ''I don't know your husband personally, but Al talks highly of him.'' He grinned. ''He talks highly of you, too, and calls your marriage 'a match made in heaven.' ''

"Coming from a hard-core cop who sees so much of the bad side of life, that's really nice," Holly said, getting to her feet. "Is it okay if I go up to Anita's room now? Umm, well, if you want to go with me, I can wait."

Joe motioned toward the food on the table he hadn't gotten to with a wave of his hand. "You go ahead. I'll stay here and enjoy." He gave her a wink. "If you come across something we overlooked, I'll start on a diet tomorrow."

Holly didn't expect to find physical evidence the Lahaina Police had overlooked, but simply believed that being in Anita Miller's room might give her some insight as to what the woman was all about. Nuances a man might disregard, yet could very well be vitally important.

With that thought in mind, Holly trudged upstairs, and let herself into the room that was so familiar to her, but now smelled of sweet pikake perfume, and resembled an island rummage sale. Every nook and cranny was filled with artificial flowers and bags and boxes containing cheap souvenirs ranging from the most outrageous—a can of "Hawaiian air"—to the most popular, shell and kukui bead necklaces, and little bottles of pikake perfume, packaged for the tourists trade with tiny artificial orchids floating inside.

There were several books scattered around, but the one Joe had mentioned was the only book that had anything to do with Hawaii. The rest were popular paperbacks, and most of them had broken spines and worn, wrinkled pages.

Holly checked the clothing in the dresser drawers and closet, but the garments only re-affirmed what Joe had told her earlier. Anita had been traveling light, and the lack of island apparel was obvious.

The lone purse was a straw-colored tote trimmed with artificial orchids, and after noting the few items it contained, Holly walked out onto the balcony, trying to rid her nostrils of the sickly sweet scent wafting through the room. Across the alley in the newly established park, several tourists were reclining on wooden benches. Remembering Stump's little white clapboard house and the lovely garden that had surrounded it, she felt her heart twist. It hadn't been much, but it had been his home.

At that moment, Stump turned into the alley from the side street, and tears filled Holly's eyes at the sight of his stooped shoulders and plodding stride. But she managed a smile, and called out, "Hi, Stump, I'm up here."

Stump managed a smile, too, but it was weary at best. When he hesitated at the bottom of the steps, Holly slipped under the yellow Mylar tape Joe had stretched across the top of the stairs, and made her way down to him. "No point in you going up there," she said, giving him a hug.

"I'll have to sooner or later," he said, sitting down on the bottom step. "I'll have to pack up her things. . . ."

Holly sat down beside him, and rested her head on his shoulder. "We can do that for you, Stump. . . . Do you know if she had any family besides her brother?"

"Al asked me the same thing, and to tell you the truth, I don't remember if she did or didn't. I vaguely remember her mentioning something about a sister, but that was back in seventy-two. A long time ago." He scuffed the tip of the peg leg in the sandy loam, and sighed. "Did you go through her things?"

"I did, for what it was worth. What about a home, Stump? Did she tell you where she was living on the mainland?"

"No, she didn't, and I didn't think to ask. ... She looked so cold, lying there in the morgue. . . ."

Holly softened her voice. "It must have been terrible for you. You were gone nearly three hours, and I was beginning to get worried."

"It didn't take all that long, actually, but then we never did get to the questions Al wanted to ask me. I was in pretty bad shape, so Al said he'd stop by later. After that, the time delay was my fault. I went for a walk. Sorry if I worried you." He heaved a sigh. "Guess I'd better get busy. It's almost time for the lunch crowd. No sign of Brent yet, huh?"

"No, but if he knows about his sister, that isn't a surprise."

Stump added, "Well, let's hope he doesn't turn up dead. Is Joe still inside?"

"He's eating lunch. . . ." At that moment, Holly caught movement out of the corner of her eye. A tall, dark-haired man had entered the alley from the side street, and was making his way toward them. Easy stride, easy smile, and quite handsome in white duck pants and a bright aloha shirt.

Stump stood up, and put out his hand.

"Hello, Ric. You're not gonna believe this, but I was actually hoping you'd stop by again. You still want a job?"

"That's why I'm here," the man said, shaking Stump's hand. But his dark eyes were on Holly, flickering down the length of her flowered sundress. "Don't remember seeing you before. Are you one of the waitresses?"

Holly was trying to decide how to answer him when Stump spoke up. "Maybe you didn't notice when you were here before, but I don't have any waitresses."

The man quirked a brow. "Well, unless my eyes are deceiving me, this pretty lady is wearing an apron, and that's an order pad clipped to the pocket. And what about that tall, sultry blond who was waiting tables when I was here before?"

Holly spoke up quickly. "I'm a good friend, and I'm helping Stump out, that's all. . . ."

"Guess I'd better tell you," Stump said. "The job I have in mind isn't for a cook. I need a bartender."

The man shrugged. "I can handle that."

Stump went on. "And I guess I'd better tell you what's going on, too. The 'tall, sultry blond' wasn't a waitress. She was my ex-wife, and somebody killed her. . . .''

The man's reaction was instant. ''Whoa, no kidding! Is that why I saw all the cops down by the wharf?''

''More than likely. They found her body in the water.''

Ric's dark eyes narrowed. ''Are you trying to tell me you're a suspect?''

Holly snapped, ''That isn't what Stump is saying at all. He simply wants you to be aware of what is going on, so you won't freak when you see the bar overflowing with cops.''

Dark eyes flashed. ''I don't *freak* at the sight of cops, lady.''

Holly lifted her chin. ''Good, because even if a murder hadn't been committed, Stump has a lot of cop friends. . . .'' She almost added, ''like my husband, who is a federal agent,'' but held back, because a guarded wariness had veiled the man's eyes, giving her a funny feeling in the pit of her stomach. Something wasn't sitting well again, some elusive *something*, and it immediately put her on guard. Anita Miller was dead, and this man was a stranger.

With a toss of her head, she said, ''I'm going inside, Stump. It's almost time for the lunch crowd, and I have to lock up Anita's room.'' She could feel the stranger's dark eyes on her as she climbed the stairs, and that wasn't sitting well, either.

In Anita's room again, Holly made one final inspection, and had just locked the balcony door when she spied the painting on the wall. She didn't remember seeing it the year before, so either Stump had added it to the decor, or it belonged to Anita. It wasn't much. A simple watercolor of some lonely harbor, and she probably would have ignored it if it hadn't been for her P.I. training. *Don't overlook the obvious.*

Moments later, Holly had the painting down, and was staring at the slip of paper that had been taped to the back. It was a list of days and times, which meant nothing at the moment, other than the fact that Anita, or somebody, had tried to hide it. And that meant everything.

A few minutes later, Holly made her way into the nearly empty bar, and the same feeling she'd had before, swept over her. Anita's so-called classy ''island decor'' was definitely hampering business, and it was time to do something about it. But, like Al was always saying, first things first.

"What do you make of this?" Holly said, joining Joe at the table. "I found it taped to the back of a painting on the wall in Anita's room."

Joe pushed aside the empty pie plate, studied the slip of paper, and frowned. "Beats me." The frown slid into a grin. "Guess this means I have to go on a diet tomorrow, huh?"

She gave him a sly wink. "Depends on who put it there, and if it has any bearing on the case. I'll show it to Stump, and see what he says. He's back, by the way. I left him in the alley, talking to the new bartender. He's assuming, of course, that Brent isn't going to show."

"Is he okay?"

"He'll be okay, and he'll be even better than that once we rid this place of Anita's influence. Look around, Joe. The bar should be full of customers and friendly locals. Instead, it's like a tomb. The place has changed so much, nobody feels at home or comfortable anymore, except for the few loyal diehards."

Cindy joined them at the table, and heaved a sigh out of complete boredom. "I heard the last of that, and I agree. Of course, I don't know what it looked like before, but *anything* would be better than this! Did you find anything interesting in Anita's room?''

"Just this strange piece of paper. It was taped to the back of a painting. Of course, we have no way of knowing if Anita put it there. . . .'' She heard Stump's peg leg hitting the floor before she turned around and smiled. "Just the man I want to see.'' She handed him the slip of paper, and explained.

Stump glanced at it, and shook his head. "I've never seen it before, and as far as the painting, Anita must have put it up.'' He looked around glumly. "I wanted to keep the bar open so I'd have something to occupy my time and mind, but now I'm beginning to wonder if that was a mistake. Hell's bells, a bomb could go off, and nobody would get hurt. We still have a fair crowd at night, and maybe that's because of the combo, but if this keeps up, I'll have to stop serving lunch.''

Holly chose her words carefully, and said, "Can you pinpoint the time when business began to drop off?''

Stump sighed. "About the time Anita made all the changes.''

"And that didn't give you some sort of a clue? I don't want to put her down, or upset you, Stump, but her taste really was in her toes, and all her changes are definitely hurting business. What would you say to closing up for a few days so we can renovate the renovations, and then you can reopen with a bang. Stump Tanner's bar and eatery as it used to be. We can even put out flyers, and. . . ."

Stump's blue eyes misted over. "Stump Tanner's, the way it used to be. You keep saying 'we.' That sounds like you're planning to give up some of your vacation time, and I can't let you do that."

Cindy admonished, "Well, that's just too bad, because Danny and I want to help out, too, so unless you want to fight all four of us . . ."

Stump waved a hand. "I know when I'm licked, but maybe you ladies had better talk to your husbands first, before making that kind of a commitment."

"Don't worry about Logan and Danny," Holly said. "They want what's best for you as much as we do. When is the bartender supposed to start work?"

"I didn't hire him after all. I could tell you didn't like him, Holly, and your instincts are good enough for me."

"I didn't necessarily dislike him," Holly returned. "It was more like a feeling that something was amiss. Still, you're definitely going to need a bartender when you reopen, so I wouldn't count him out. Do you know how to get in touch with him if you change your mind?"

"Yeah, I do. He's renting a room behind the pizzeria a few blocks down."

It was at that moment, Holly got the brainstorm, and it was a good one. "What about Lila? Do you think she would come back?"

Stump shrugged. "I can't answer that, because I don't know why she left."

"Well, maybe I can find out," Holly said with enthusiasm. "Does she live in Lahaina?"

"She lives up by the old cemetery on Shaw Street. That's just off Wainee."

"Is it within walking distance?"

"It is, for somebody with your youthful exuberance. Now, I suppose you want the address?"

"If you don't mind."

"I don't mind, and if you can get Lila to come back, I'd be eternally grateful."

Holly got up and gave Stump a hug. "Then

it's settled. While I'm gone, be thinking about the best time to close down for a few days."

Joe reached under his shirt, and pulled a portable radio from his belt. "You want a ride? I can have a unit here in a few minutes."

"I'd love a ride, if it isn't too much trouble. The sooner I can get there, the sooner I can get back."

He keyed the mike. "Consider it done."

Because she didn't want to pull up in front of Lila's house in a patrol car, Holly asked the nice-looking officer to let her out a block from the house, and made arrangements to meet him at the same corner a half hour later. And now, as she made her way up the flower-lined pathway, she was glad she did, because Lila was sitting on the front porch, reading a book.

She was a beautiful woman, with long, black hair, and although she was probably in her mid to late forties, her figure, accentuated by a pair of shorts and a T-shirt, was lithe and lovely. And her smile was as bright as the Hawaiian sun.

"Hi, Lila," Holly greeted her. "I don't know if you remember me, but . . ."

"I don't remember your name," Lila returned, "but I remember your face and red hair. You're one of Stump's friends. You're a private detective, and . . ." She snapped her fingers. "You and your husband stayed in a room above the bar about a year ago, right?"

"That's right. Holly and Logan West. We were on our honeymoon. Now, we're celebrating our first anniversary."

Lila's pretty mouth turned down. "Well, I don't envy you if you're staying at the bar." She waved a hand toward a white rattan chair. "Sit down, please. I just made some lemonade. . . ."

"Thanks, Lila, but I'll pass on the lemonade. I know you left your job unexpectedly, and without giving Stump notice. Was there a reason for that?"

Lila snapped, "Why don't you ask his blond guest? I'm sure she would be more than happy to tell you." Her dark eyes lowered, and her cheeks flushed pink. "I'm sorry. That was rude, and uncalled for."

"You don't have to apologize, Lila, because I understand. Anita Miller affected me that way, too." Holly took a deep breath. "Anita was killed sometime last night or early this morning. Her body was found in the water near the wharf. . . ."

Stricken, Lila exclaimed, "The *haolewahine* is *make*, dead?"

"Yes," Holly replied. "Somebody shot her through the heart."

Lila shivered as tears filled her eyes. "Poor Stump. He must be overwhelmed with grief!"

"I won't deny he's upset, but some things have come to light that have put Anita's visit into a different perspective, and now we're left with dozens of unanswered questions."

"And you're hoping I can answer them? I knew very little about her, other than the fact she was Stump's ex-wife, and popped up unexpectedly. At first, I thought it was a good thing, you know? Stump seemed so pleased to see her, but then . . . Well, it wasn't long before I realized she was trying to take over Stump and the bar, and make the bar into something it was never meant to be. The more time that went on, the angrier I became, until one night, she forced the issue, and I finally had it out with her."

"Was that inside the bar?" Holly asked.

"No. I was on my break, and I'd gone outside to get a breath of fresh air. She followed me, and demanded I stop filling Stump's head with wicked lies. It wasn't true, of course. No matter what I thought of her, I never once told Stump how I felt. I didn't think it was my place to say anything derogatory about her, for one thing, but more important, I didn't want to hurt him." She flushed again, and looked away.

"Because you love him?" Holly said softly.

Lila managed a smile. "Because I love him, only he doesn't know how I feel."

"But Anita knew, and thought of you as a threat?"

"She didn't say that in so many words, but she did say that she planned to stay on in Lahaina indefinitely, that Stump belonged to her, and that she would see to it he fired me. I tried to tell her I'd been working at the bar for several years, that I loved my job and Stump would never fire me without a reason, and that's when she announced that unless I quit immediately, like that very night, she would see to it he had a reason. I didn't believe her, and refused. The next night, my cash drawer came up fifty dollars short. I replaced the money with my own, and walked out. I knew I couldn't fight a woman like her, and that the missing money would only be the beginning."

"Why didn't you tell Stump about that conversation, Lila?"

"Because he was so wrapped up in his 'honeybunch,' I knew he wouldn't believe me. That happened a couple of weeks ago, and I still haven't been able to go out and look for another job. I'll have to give the bar as a reference, and I've been afraid of the outcome."

"Do you live here alone?" Holly asked.

"I have a daughter and a son. Both teenagers, and typically demanding. I desperately need the income, and yet, here I sit. I've never been the kind of woman who's intimidated easily, but Anita Miller really got to me."

"Would you consider coming back now? Stump said if I could talk you into it, he'd be eternally grateful."

"Because he needs a bartender," she said dismally.

"He also needs your friendship," Holly offered.

"What did he do for a bartender after I left?"

"Anita had a brother, only Stump didn't know he was her brother. Shortly after you left, the brother walked in, and was hired on the spot. Now, the brother is missing. We believe he either killed her, knows who killed her and is on the run, or he's met with foul play, too.''

Lila squared her shoulders. ''When does Stump want me to begin?''

Holly gave Lila a warm smile, and it reflected the relief she felt. ''I think it would be best if you talk to Stump about any long-range plans, because he's going to close the bar for a few days so we can remedy Anita's renovations, but I know for a fact the bar will be open tonight.''

''Then I'll start tonight. Tell him I'll be there around three so we'll have time to talk, and then if he still wants me. . . .''

Holly reached over and gave Lila's hand a squeeze. ''I wouldn't worry about that, Lila. And just between the two of us, the sooner the bar gets back to some sort of normalcy, the better off he'll be.

''Aloha. Until this afternoon . . .''

''Aloha,'' Lila returned, with a little catch in her voice.

The police officer was waiting for Holly when she reached the corner a few minutes later, and the smile on her face was radiant.

Stump had closed his heart to love years ago, but she had the feeling that was about to change. And maybe they could even have a happy ending. . . .

Chapter Five

It was late afternoon before Logan walked into the bar, and Holly knew by the defeated slump to his shoulders the trip to Lanai had been a bust.

"Nobody remembered seeing Anita or the brother," Logan said, plopping down on a barstool, "and we covered every inch of the island." He looked around and frowned. "Do I dare ask what's going on?"

"If you're talking about the lack of customers," Holly said, handing him a tall glass of iced tea, "Stump decided to close down for a couple of days so we can make renovations on

84

the renovations. Didn't you see the notice out front?''

''To tell you the truth, I didn't. So, is that why you're wearing grubbies, and all the plants and furniture have been moved out?''

''That's right, my love. Stump will still have to use the new tables because they were such an expensive investment, but once we pull up the Astroturf and get rid of all the artificial flowers, it shouldn't look too bad. Fortunately, he saved the tapa wallpaper that was behind the bar, along with those wonderful old drawings of the waterfront.''

''So, where is everybody?''

''You first. Where is Danny?''

''He stayed on the *Sea Breeze* to freshen up. Your turn.''

''Tutu and Tonoa are in the kitchen, doing whatever they have to do to prepare for a two-day closure, Stump is out in the alley, talking to Al, and Cindy and Lila are upstairs, packing Anita's things in boxes.''

Logan raised a brow. ''Lila?''

Holly gave him a dimpled grin. ''The pretty dark-haired bartender. I went to see her this afternoon, and she agreed to come back to work. It didn't take much when she found out about Anita.''

"Then we were right. Anita forced her to leave.''

"In a most unsettling way. It really upset Lila, because she admitted she's in love with Stump. He doesn't know it, of course, and how she handles it is her business, but I have the feeling Lila's love is just what he needs right about now.''

"How is he? I mean, it couldn't have been easy viewing Anita's body.''

"He took it pretty hard, but he'll be okay. Oh, I met Ric today. You know, the guy who claims he's another Wolfgang Puck. Actually, Stump offered him the bartender's job and he was going to take it, but then Stump changed his mind because he sensed my wariness. There was something about him that didn't ring true, only don't ask me to explain it, because I can't. Anyway, that's why I went to talk to Lila, and I'm really glad I did.''

"No sign of the brother, huh?''

"No, and it certainly gives a curious edge to the situation, wondering if he's dead or alive.''

"Sounds like your day was more exciting than ours."

"It wasn't necessarily exciting, but it was productive. Oh, I also found a slip of paper taped to the back of a picture in Anita's room. It was a list of dates and times. Stump said the picture belonged to Anita, so we have to assume it was her list. Al has it now, though he can't make much sense of it, either."

"Are the dates current?" Logan asked.

"It's hard to say, because there was no mention of the month or year. But the fact she had it hidden behind a picture certainly sounds suspicious, along with a few other things, like her lack of island clothing, and the fact we couldn't find identification of any kind."

"Sounds like she was traveling light and anonymously."

"That's what Joe said."

Logan frowned. "Joe?"

"Sergeant Joe Kaloni."

"Ah, otherwise known as Pupule Mauna."

"And he really is as big as a mountain. He's also a very nice man. He's off duty now, and his replacement should be here soon. But back to Anita. For somebody who was traveling light, her room was full of boxes and bags packed with cheap souvenirs.''

"That doesn't sound so strange, Holly. Tourists buy cheap souvenirs all the time if they are on a limited budget.''

"Yes, but in large quantities? What would a person want with one hundred shell necklaces or kukui beads? I didn't actually count them, but I'd say that's a close guess.''

Logan finished the iced tea, and shrugged. "Maybe a friend had a gift shop that needed stocking.''

"So she buys the stuff retail when the friend could get it wholesale? I don't think so, Logan. She also had a jillion bottles of pikake perfume. The room reeked of it, yet I don't remember Anita wearing that particular fragrance.''

"Did you talk to Stump about it?''

"Not yet, but I will. You look exhausted, my love. Have you eaten?''

"We had lunch at one of the hotels. You?''

"I had a bowl of soup, and ate every drop. Did you get by to see Tutu's family?''

"Didn't have the time.'' He wrapped his arms around her, and sighed. "This isn't the way I wanted to celebrate our anniversary, sweetheart.''

Holly snuggled close. ''I know, but we'll make up for it later. Right now, Stump needs our help.''

''And that's what friends are for,'' Logan said, kissing the tip of her nose. He looked down at the Astroturf. ''Might as well begin ripping it up. I don't know about you, but I can't wait to see the old marred wooden floor.''

Holly was anxious to have the bar restored to its original condition, too, but her concern went far beyond the old wooden floor and a few rolls of tapa wallpaper. Until Anita's killer was apprehended, nothing could really be the same. . . .

''Hi, Logan. Where's Danny?'' Cindy asked, coming down the stairs two at a time.

''He should be along shortly,'' Logan replied. ''He wanted to freshen up.''

''Any luck on Lanai?''

''I'll let Danny tell you about it, but suffice to say, it was a wasted trip.''

Lila was behind Cindy, carrying a box, and her eyes crossed in disgust. ''This box contains all those little bottles of cheap pikake, and I'll

never get the scent out of my nostrils! We
stopped counting at fifty.'' She put the box on
the bar, and smiled at Logan. ''It's Logan
West, right? I never forget a handsome face.''

Logan returned her smile. ''And I never forget a pretty face. It's good to see you again.''

Cindy stretched her arms over her head. ''If
you guys don't mind, I'm going to the boat. I
haven't seen my handsome husband all day,
and . . .''

Logan chuckled. ''Say no more.''

After Cindy left, Lila sighed. ''Young love.
Isn't it wonderful?''

Holly said gently, ''Love is wonderful at any
age. Just ask those two in the kitchen!''

Lila sighed dreamily. ''Tutu and Tonoa.
Even the names go together. Is Stump
around?''

Holly nodded. ''The last time I saw him, he
was out in the alley talking to Al Gainer.''

''I'm right here, and I'm all talked out,''
Stump said, wearily plodding into the bar. He
waved a hand at Logan. ''Hello, mate. Any
luck on Lanai?''

''No, unfortunately. Did Al leave?''

''Yeah, he did. He said he was gonna be the
recipient of flying pots and pans if he didn't

make it home for dinner. Speaking of dinner, sandwiches will be the bill of fare, but Tutu still wants a head count.''

''You're looking at it,'' Logan said. ''Cindy and Danny are on the boat, and I don't think we'll see them again tonight.''

Stump managed a grin. ''Mushy stuff.'' He winked at Lila. ''You wanted to talk to me, pretty lady?''

Lila pointed at the box on the bar. ''I just wanted to know if I could take this particular box out to the alley. It's packed full of bottles of pikake perfume we found in Anita's room, and I can still smell the strong scent even through the cardboard.''

Stump frowned. ''Yeah, sure, I don't care, but it's mighty strange. Anita didn't wear perfume. She was allergic to the stuff.''

''Maybe she bought it to give as gifts?'' Logan reasoned.

Holly returned, ''Then why does her room reek of pikake?''

''Reek? You mean, like she opened the bottles?''

''Opened them and spilled out the contents, would be more to the point,'' Lila said, making a face. ''I left the outside door open, Stump, along with the window, but I closed the inner door to the hallway. Hopefully the room will eventually air out so you won't have the stench through the whole bar.''

''Mighty strange,'' Stump repeated, scratching his head. ''But then so was her murder, and her brother's disappearance.'' He hoisted the box. ''I'll take the box out to the alley, pretty lady. I have to give Tutu the head count anyway.''

After he'd gone, Lila gave a heartfelt sigh. ''He looks like he's aged ten years, and I feel so helpless.''

''We all feel helpless,'' Holly admitted, ''but at least we're here for him if he needs us.

''Now, I'm going to start on the floor, because the sooner we get rid of this fake grass, the happier I'll be.''

A few minutes later, as Holly, Logan, and Lila made plans to work on the indoor/outdoor carpeting in assembly-line fashion, Cindy rushed in, nearly hysterical. ''Danny wasn't on the boat!'' she cried. ''And it looks like there was a fight!''

Trying to get Cindy to calm down, Logan gave her a gentle shake. ''Fight? What kind of a fight, Cindy?''

"You know. Stuff scattered all over everywhere. . . . Oh, Logan, if anything has happened to Danny . . ."

"The *Sea Breeze* is a good-sized vessel, Cindy. Did you look everywhere?"

"No. I called his name but he didn't answer me, and then I saw the mess. . . ."

Logan grabbed up the phone, and punched in the numbers. Within seconds he was explaining to the police what had happened, and how he wanted to handle it.

Holly could only hear Logan's side of the conversation, but there was no mistaking his request. He was going to the *Sea Breeze*, and wanted the police to meet him there.

By the time they reached the *Sea Breeze*, several police units had arrived, along with Al Gainer, who had gotten the page just as he was sitting down to dinner. Logan had wanted Holly to stay behind, but hadn't argued with her, knowing he would be wasting his breath.

Searching the *Sea Breeze* had been pointless, too, for there was no sign of Danny anywhere. And now, standing on the deck with Logan and Al, listening to the voices and laughter coming from a yacht moored three slips down, Holly shook her head in despair. "This is a total nightmare! From the way everything is strewn around, I'd say it was an attempted robbery, and Danny got in the way."

Al shoved his hands in his pockets. "Which is exactly why I got in touch with the Harbor Patrol. They are going to drag the harbor. If Danny got in the way of the burglar, I don't think he was abducted. More than likely he was knocked out, or worse, and tossed overboard. You said Danny stayed behind to freshen up. Maybe the crook saw you leave, Logan, and figured nobody else was on board."

Holly shivered uncontrollably, even though the early-evening air was warm. Between the *Sea Breeze* and the boat full of partygoers, a yacht named *Sweet Alice* sat in silent repose. On the other side, the slip was empty. "Maybe we should talk to the people over there," she said, pointing at the party boat.

"I have two men over there now," Al said. "For what it's worth. They are in their own little booze-filled world, and probably didn't see a thing." He sighed, and looked at Logan. "Could you tell if anything is missing?"

"Not that I could see," Logan replied. "But

then the only things on board of value are locked up. Danny is a big man, Al, and he knows how to handle himself. He would have had to have been taken completely by surprise for the creep to get the upper hand.''

Holly felt her heart twist. ''I can't tell Cindy they are going to drag the harbor. . . .''

''No, but you can tell her the police are doing everything they can to find him. I think you should go back to the bar, sweetheart. You should be with Cindy.''

''I know,'' Holly said dejectedly. ''But it's all so sad, I can hardly stand it. This is supposed to be their honeymoon. . . .'' Holly's words trailed off, and she squared her shoulders. She had never been a pessimist, and she wasn't going to start now.

After giving Logan a kiss and a hug, she headed for the bar, trying to draw in the kind of strength she would need to help her dear friend.

Holly had reached the alleyway behind the bait and tackle shop when she heard the moan. And then another, along with a string of curses. She recognized the voice, and with her heart pounding in her chest, cried out, ''Danny, is that you! Oh, Danny, where are you?''

The answer was music to her ears. "I'm in the alley, covered with fish heads, sawdust, and brine. When I get the name of the truck driver who ran me down, I'll let you know."

Danny was trying to make light of his harrowing experience, and tears filled Holly's eyes. He was alive and, at the moment, that was all that mattered.

Chapter Six

With colorful lanterns strung up on the overhead beams and tall candles ablaze on the table, the veranda looked more than festive. But then everybody was smiling, too. Even Danny, who was nursing one king-size head-ache. Stump had suggested they wait until to-morrow to begin work on the bar, and nobody had objected.

By the time they'd eaten Tutu's chicken salad sandwiches, and were on a second pot of coffee, Danny had finished giving Al the de-tails of his incredible story, and this time, Al was taking notes.

"So you caught the culprit in the act, and he ran," Al said. "Can you describe him?"

Danny shrugged. "Not enough to be much help, I'm afraid. He was wearing a fisherman's hat pulled down over his ears, and I only got a glimpse of the side of his face. Dark complexion. Possibly an islander or a *haole* with a tan."

"Clothes?" Al asked.

"Jeans and a gray sweatshirt. White deck shoes. I remember he had big feet and big hands. It happened so fast, it's still a blur."

"Did you see him when he came on board?" Logan asked.

Cindy was holding his hand, and he kissed her fingers. It was a comforting gesture, and filled with love. "No, I didn't. I was in the head and when I came out, there he was. Before I could get my mind or feet in gear, he was gone. I was on my way to the bar when he came out of nowhere, and the next thing I knew, I was waking up in the alley, and Holly was having a screaming fit."

Holly said, "You were moaning, Danny, otherwise I would have walked right on by."

Danny touched the back of his head gingerly. "I didn't see anything in his hands, so I have no idea what he hit me with."

"The alley was full of garbage and debris," Logan offered, "so it could have been anything, though I have the feeling it was the butt of a gun. I still think you should go to the hospital and let them check you out."

"No way. Hospitals and I don't get along. Besides, it would take more than a lump on the head to do me under."

Stump spoke up, and weighed his words carefully. "I know you're a big, strapping man, Danny, and security is your business, but I think you should consider staying in the room upstairs tonight."

"I've already considered it," Danny replied. "Even though Al said he'd put a cop on the *Sea Breeze*, I'm not in any hurry to go back. And I know Cindy would feel safer here."

Stump nodded. "Say no more. I'll go up and make sure the room is ready."

"I'll go with you," Lila said, giving Stump a warm smile. "There are still quite a few boxes in Anita's room, so maybe you can give me a hand?" She cast her dark eyes downward. "I'm sorry, Stump. That was thoughtless on my part. . . ."

"Don't worry about it," he said, returning her smile. "I have to face that room sooner or later, and it might as well be now."

After they'd gone, Holly sighed. "Lila is happy to be back, and Stump is happy to have her back. Maybe this will be a new beginning for them." She looked at Danny's puzzled expression, and smiled. "Lila is in love with Stump, only he doesn't know it."

"Then Anita *did* see Lila as a threat and was responsible for getting rid of her?"

"That's right. No doubt Anita could see the love in Lila's eyes, even if Stump couldn't. But I have the feeling all that's about to change."

Danny settled back in his chair, and winked at his wife. "Love has a way of making everything right.

"So, how about bringing me up to date? Sounds like a lot happened while we were gone. I'm sure Logan has told you about our misadventures on Lanai. . . ."

"Misadventures?" Holly queried, raising a brow.

Logan cleared his throat. "Umm, well, we sort of got into an altercation with the guy at the car rental place. He told us how to get to Lanai City, but he was wrong, and we ended up at Shipwreck Beach.'' He smiled at Cindy. ''Unless you've been on Lanai, it's hard to understand how you can get lost on such a small island. For starters, there are only a few paved roads, and none of them are marked. I knew we were in trouble the minute we ran out of pavement.''

Holly rolled her eyes. ''So you called the guy a jerk when you returned the car, and he took personal offense?''

''We didn't call him a jerk, but we did tell him his mistake cost us a lot of additional miles, and that translates into extra money in his pocket.''

''Didn't he give you a map?'' Holly asked.

Danny smirked. ''He was conveniently out of them. Is that a surprise, or what?''

''Sounds like a scam to me,'' Cindy said.

Logan nodded. ''And that's what we basically told him.''

Al had his notebook crammed with unanswered questions, and pointed at one in particular. ''This question seems to be the biggie. Was the guy who assaulted Danny on the *Sea*

Breeze a thief? Or is the incident connected to the murder?''

Holly asked, ''Have you had any other break-ins or robberies at the wharf?''

''None that I know of or that have been reported. We had an incident at one of the hotels a few months back, but those things can happen anywhere.'' He stood up, and tucked the notebook in a pocket. ''Guess I'll check in with my men down on the wharf. Don't expect they've come up with anything by talking to the people on the neighboring boats, but I can always hope. And you never know—'' He broke off as Stump hurried out on the veranda, flailing his arms and fuming. Lila was right behind him, and her face was pale and drawn.

''Those steps from the balcony to the alley are coming down first thing in the morning,'' Stump announced heatedly. ''Somebody was in Anita's room, and took all the boxes.''

Lila sank to a chair and heaved a sigh. ''It's my fault. I left the door to the balcony open so the room would air out.''

Stump gave Lila's shoulder a comforting squeeze. ''It's not your fault, pretty lady.''

''The brother?'' Logan queried.

Al shrugged, and whipped his portable radio

off his duty belt. "Maybe. I'll get a couple of men over here to dust for prints again. Maybe this time we'll luck out."

Holly gazed out at the harbor where the reflection of the full Hawaiian moon danced across the water. "Maybe that man was aboard the *Sea Breeze* because he was looking for something. Something that was right here in Anita's room all along. The whole thing is connected to Anita's murder, Logan. I can *feel* it."

Cindy spoke up, and the tone in her voice turned heads. "What about the box Stump took out to the alley this afternoon? I mean, maybe the culprit overlooked it, and . . ."

Now, all eyes were on Stump, whose rugged face broke into a a sly grin. "I didn't take it out to the alley. When I told Tonoa what I was going to do with it, he suggested—if the ultimate end was to eventually throw it out—I put the box in the storage room, because his sister likes that brand of pikake perfume."

Before Stump had the words out of his mouth, Logan was on his way to the storage room, leaving them all with a great deal of hope that at least a small part of the mystery might finally be solved.

*   *   *

"Diamonds," Logan said, looking down at the glittering gems Al held in his hand.

Lila hadn't disturbed the smaller box full of bottles of pikake perfume, but had simply placed it in a larger box, and filled it with loose beads, shell necklaces, and novelties before taping the lid shut. Al had found the cache of diamonds in the smaller box under the excelsior used for packing, and estimated they were worth a good two hundred thousand, if not more. They also suggested a diamond robbery, and left everyone a little breathless, but also put a few of the puzzle pieces in place.

Logan finally said the words they were all thinking. "I'd say Anita and her brother were part of a diamond heist, and that's why they were on the run."

"I think it's much more involved than that," Holly said thoughtfully. "They might have been running from the police, but what if there was a third party involved? What if they skipped out on that person, and that person finally found them? If that person knew they had the diamonds, it might explain Anita's death, the brother's disappearance, and the theft of Anita's things.''

"It might explain why she had so many boxes and bags full of gift items, too," Logan offered. "If they were all packed with excelsior." He nodded at the diamonds. "You realize this might be only the tip of the iceberg."

Stump sat down wearily, and put his chin in his hands. ''No matter how she found out I had a bar in Lahaina, she probably figured I'd be a good patsy, and this would be a good place to hide out. Good old unsuspecting Stump Tanner to the rescue.''

Danny spoke up. "Then it's possible the incident on the *Sea Breeze* was just that. An isolated incident.''

Logan nodded. "Because even if the perp was watching us and knew we were friends with Stump, there would be no reason at all to believe we had the diamonds.''

Al returned the diamonds to the box and closed the lid. "I'll go to my office and do some checking. If there was a diamond heist, it has to be logged in somewhere.''

"What if it happened on the mainland?" Cindy asked.

"It might take a little longer, that's all.

Meanwhile, I'll keep a man staked out in the park across the alley, and one in an unmarked unit out front. Keep your eyes open and your backs covered. We still have a killer at large, and we don't have a clue to his identity. And that makes me nervous.''

It made Holly nervous, too, and had put her mind on overload. ''Do you suppose the list of dates and times I found taped behind the painting had something to do with the diamonds?''

Al shrugged, and tucked the box under his arm. ''I dunno, but that's one of the questions on my list. I'll stop by in the morning. Hopefully by then I'll have some answers.''

After Al had gone, Stump sighed wearily. ''The room upstairs is ready, though I don't suppose anybody is gonna get much sleep tonight.''

''I'd better go home before my kids think I ran out on them,'' Lila said, getting to her feet. ''In light of what's happening, do you still want to work on the renovations tomorrow?''

''Pulling up Astroturf is the last thing on my mind,'' Stump muttered. ''But I suppose it would be better that sitting around, twiddling our thumbs.''

"Yes, it would," Holly agreed. "And the sooner we're done, the sooner you can reopen."

"There's safety in numbers, so I'll walk you home," Stump said, giving Lila a wan smile.

"And for that reason, we'll make it a three-some," Logan offered.

Nobody objected.

Twenty minutes later, Holly was sitting at the bar listing the things that had happened in chronological order, hoping to find a clue, when Ric walked through the open front door.

Because Cindy and Danny had retired for the night, Tutu was still in the kitchen with Tonoa, the cop hadn't arrived out front, and Holly hadn't changed her mind about the handsome stranger, she not only felt vulnerable, but very much alone.

"This is a bummer," Ric drawled, looking around the empty room. "I was all set for a tall, cool one, and a little music."

"We're in the middle of renovations," Holly said, taking in his crisp tan pants and expensive silk aloha shirt. She hadn't noticed before, but he was also wearing a Rolex watch and a diamond ring on his pinky finger. Hardly the type who would be willing to take a job as a cook or bartender. Or the type who would be renting a room behind a pizza parlor. She also noted his dark complexion, large hands and feet, and the fact he was wearing white deck shoes. Coincidence? Or . . .

"I thought the renovations were finished," he said, sliding up on the barstool beside her.

Holly took a deep breath, and tried to keep her voice relaxed. "They were, but Stump decided to make some additional changes. Umm, if you're here about the job, it's been filled."

His dark eyes roamed over her. "I just said I came for a tall, cool one, and a little island music. I knew earlier today I wasn't going to get the job.

"So, what about you? You said you were a friend of Stump's and you were helping him out. I also noticed your wedding ring. Is your hubby helping out, too?"

Torn between telling him Logan was a cop, which might scare him away, and breezing over it so she could get as much information as possible, she chose the latter. "He's helping out. He's upstairs in our room, but he should be down any minute."

He looked around. "And Stump?"

"He's probably in the kitchen. . . . Uh, I know your name is Ric, but I don't think I caught your last name."

His smile was easy, though guarded. "It's Brown; what's yours? Come to think of it, I don't even know your first name. If you'll recall, we weren't introduced."

Anita Miller, *Brent* Smith, *and now Ric* Brown. *Convenient, nondescript last names*, Holly noted to herself. "It's Holly St. James," she said, deciding to keep Logan's name out of it.

"Do you live around here?"

"On one of the neighboring islands."

"Did you fly over?"

Not wanting to tell him about the *Sea Breeze*, Holly answered his question with a question. "What about you, Mr. Brown? Stump said you're renting a room behind the pizzeria, but I have the feeling you aren't an islander."

"Why do you say that?" he asked nonchalantly.

"Because I can usually spot a *haole* mainlander a block away."

"*Haole*. What does that mean?"

"It means Caucasian. That's opposed to a *kama'aina*, or native-born islander. Everybody in the islands knows what a *haole* is, so I guess that answers my question."

His dark eyes flickered with interest. "You're not only beautiful, you're observant. I've also noticed how you phrase your questions. Are you a cop?"

His question surprised her, but didn't throw her off guard. "No, I'm not a cop. So, where are you from, Mr. Brown?"

"I've lived all over the world at one time or another, but this is my first time in Hawaii."

"Then you plan on staying?"

"Maybe, if I find it to my liking."

Evasive, mysterious, and arrogant, she thought to herself. Knowing she should stall until Logan and Stump returned, but knowing it was a moot thought because she had nothing at all that could prove Ric was the killer, and certainly nothing that would warrant taking him to the police station for questioning, Holly said quickly, "I'm going to lock up now, Mr. Brown. If you want a 'tall, cool one' and to listen to island music, I suggest you come back after we've finished the renovations."

He shrugged, slid off the barstool, and headed for the door, tossing over his shoulder, "*Ahui ho*, Holly St. James."

Holly stared after him, and felt a chill sweep down her back. *Ahui ho* meant "Until we meet again," and yet he'd said he'd never been to Hawaii before, and wasn't even familiar with the common term *haole*.

A few minutes later, Holly was on the phone with Al, sounding like a befuddled schoolgirl instead of a private detective. Her words sounded jumbled, even to her own ears, and she had a hard time catching her breath.

After a few moments, Al chided, "Come on, Holly, slow down! You say he was wearing white deck shoes, has big feet and hands, and he was evasive about his background. That's hardly enough to have him picked up for questioning."

"I know, but it was more than that," Holly reasoned, going on to explain about the discrepancy in the language. "He didn't even know what *haole* meant, for Pete's sake, and then he comes up with '*Ahui ho*'? And don't forget, he did pop up looking for a job about the same time Anita and her brother arrived on the island. I know, Anita didn't appear to know him, but then it's possible she wouldn't know the person who was after them, and that goes for the brother, too.''

"I don't know, Holly. If they were on the run, I would think every stranger would be suspect.''

"Then other than Stump, everybody on Maui would be suspect, so I would think the *last* place they would want to hide out was in a bar as popular as Stump Tanner's. I know, I'm contradicting myself, but you didn't see him, Al. Oh, and he was wearing a Rolex watch and a diamond ring, too, not to mention his tailor-made silk aloha shirt. Does that sound like a man who would settle for a job as a cook or a bartender?''

"Maybe he's the type who likes to put on a big show,'' Al asserted. "That doesn't make him a killer.'' There was a long pause, and then, "Well, hell's bells, Holly. You're a good P.I., and I know from experience your instincts are good. Okay, I'll put a tail on him, and we'll go from there. That's about all I can do, under the circumstances. Too bad Stump didn't give him the job. That way you could be keeping an eye on him, too.'' He cleared his throat.

"Scratch that. Too much risk if he's the killer."

Holly agreed it was a risk, but a plan was already forming in her mind. Tinker, tailor, cowboy, sailor. Killer or innocent *haole*. Only time would tell.

Chapter Seven

By ten o'clock the next morning, with Lila and Tutu's help, they had stripped away the Astroturf, replaced the tapa paper on the wall behind the bar, Hedy Lamarr was up, Betty Grable was down, and fresh flowers adorned all the tables. Stump still hadn't gotten around to dismantling the balcony steps, but it was next on their agenda. Because they'd accomplished so much, and the bar was beginning to look like the old Stump Tanner's bar and eatery again, the mood should have been festive. Unfortunately, they'd stayed up very late discussing the case and making decisions, and apprehension filled the air. If Ric Brown

114

popped up again, Stump was going to offer him a job as a waiter, and suggest he move into Anita's room. Al had contended that if Ric Brown was responsible for taking Anita's boxes, he'd probably refuse both the job and the room, because what would be the point? But Holly had taken it one step further, and had won the debate. If Ric Brown was the killer and/or the thief, why was he sticking around? It had to be much more important than wanting to drink a "tall, cool one" and to listen to island music. Like maybe there was something that hadn't been in the boxes? Something he still believed was in the bar or in Anita's room? If she was right, Ric would no doubt jump at Stump's offer, proving her point. It would also put their lives in jeopardy, Al had asserted. But his argument had fallen on deaf ears.

By noontime, everybody was so edgy, Logan finally called Al to see if the tail he'd put on Ric had come up with anything. Unfortunately, the tail had been sitting in his unit all morning watching the pizzeria, because Ric hadn't left the establishment. Al said he would call back in an hour with an update, but he didn't, and as one hour stretched into two, emotions jangled and nerves frayed.

"Something has happened," Holly finally said, attempting to choke down one of the dried-out sandwiches Tonoa had prepared for lunch, and nobody had bothered to eat.

"Something happened all right," Al said, plodding into the bar. "Sorry I didn't call sooner, but . . . Well . . ." He sat down on a barstool, and all eyes were on him. "Ric Brown is dead."

Stunned, they stared at Al.

"Only his name wasn't Ric Brown," Al went on. "It was Richard Morgan. He was a Federal agent. He and his partner, Bud Pearson, have been working on the case for months. The trail took them all over the mainland, and finally led them to the islands. Specifically, Lanai."

Logan frowned. "We covered every inch of Lanai and didn't find a trace of Anita or her brother."

Al offered, "That's because they were renting a room in a private house, and rarely went out. When they did, it was only to shop for groceries, using the chuggedy old truck that was at their disposal. And, as I understand it, they usually went in disguise. Seems the agents managed to get a room close by, and had them under surveillance.''

Holly heaved a giant sigh. "Let me guess. The case the agents were working on had something to do with a diamond heist, right?''

"That's right, and it was major big-time. A gang consisting of a dozen players, who knocked off diamond marts and jewelry stores from New York to L.A. Anita and her brother were part of the group of twenty carriers. Their job was to carry diamonds to designated places around the mainland, meet with the fences, get the money, and turn it over to the big boys, after which they would get their cut.''

Logan shook his head. "Only this time, Anita and her brother decided to keep the diamonds they were carrying for themselves.''

"That's right, and these particular diamonds were a part of the ultimate heist. Megabucks. The feds, with help from the L.A.P.D., busted the case wide open two months ago, and rounded up most of the players, sans the diamonds.''

Danny made a face. "Rounded up everybody with the exception of Anita and her brother.''

"With the exception of Anita and her brother. At least that's what they thought. But now that Anita and Agent Morgan are dead, it puts a new wrinkle in things if, in fact, the brother isn't the killer. Simply put, it means somebody else has been tracking them, and found them. Agent Pearson has a team of cops watching the house on Lanai in the event Brent shows up there, and he's on his way to Maui. Meanwhile, feds are on their way from Oahu and the mainland."

"Feds like Eliot Ness, o' wot?" Tutu said, giving them a grin.

Her comment finally brought smiles around.

"Did you tell him Logan is a semiretired fed?" Stump asked Al.

"I did, but he didn't seem impressed. But then, he was pretty upset. The thing is, they knew who they were after with the brother and sister, and once they located them, it was easy to keep them under surveillance. And they planned to keep them under surveillance until they were sure Anita and Brent were working alone. After that, they planned to make the arrest. Case closed. But then Anita made the move to Maui, and Brent followed a few weeks later. Only they hadn't given up the room on

Lanai, so the agents assumed they would be coming back. That's why the agents decided to split up.''

Stump said, ''So one agent kept watch on the house on Lanai, and the other agent followed them here. Sounds like Anita was telling the truth when she said she heard about my bar while she was on Lanai.''

Al nodded. ''More than likely. Probably decided to try your bar on for size before making the permanent move. It also explains why they were traveling light. They left most of their stuff in the room on Lanai which, by the way, contained nothing of value. Meaning no diamonds or contraband.''

Holly finished the sandwich, and washed it down with a soda before she said, ''I can see why Agent Morgan wanted a job at the bar. And it was smart. He would've been right under Anita and Brent's unsuspecting noses. But something is really bothering me. I'm married to a fed. Most of Logan's close friends are feds, or are in some type of law enforcement. Oh, I know, he *is* DEA, but a fed is a fed is a fed, and a cop is a cop is a cop. Meaning they all have a certain look, and I've always been able to tell. But that man—Agent Morgan—

was just the opposite. I didn't particularly like him, and I didn't have a clue.''

Al gave her a lopsided grin. ''Sounds to me like he was one good undercover agent.''

''How did Agent Morgan die?'' Logan asked.

''Shot at close range down near the wharf. Time of death was probably sometime late last night. Before I put the unit on the pizzeria. Nobody heard or saw anything, so the killer no doubt used a silencer. If so, it was a professional hit. The bullet is at Ballistics now, and they'll compare it to the bullet that killed Anita. It's a good thing he was carrying ID and had Agent Pearson's phone number on Lanai in his room, or it would've really slowed things down.''

Tutu stood up and smoothed down her muumuu. ''Feds are coming, so there must be food ready. Lots of food. Big turkey. Big ham. Big fish, and sweets. Cops like sweets and lots of coffee.''

Al couldn't help but smile. ''It sounds like Logan and his friends have been pretty good teachers, Tutu. Um, we might as well make the bar the command post, if you don't mind, Stump.''

"I was going to suggest it," Stump said. "The cops won't be able to find lodging in Lahaina without reservations this time of year, and I wasn't planning on reopening until next Saturday. We can round up cots and sleeping bags, and set the bar up like a dorm."

Al scratched his chin. "Saturday is five days away. I don't know, Stump. If this isn't wrapped up by then . . ."

Stump raised a hand. "If it isn't, it isn't."

Logan spoke up. "The agents will pay their way. The *Sea Breeze* will be available, too, if there is any overflow. I don't know how many agents we're talking about here, but a cop killer always brings them out of the woodwork."

"Cop killer" had such an ominous ring to it, Holly found herself shivering.

Logan gave her a hug, and Stump an apologetic smile. "Seems like every time we hit the island, you end up in the middle of a mess, Stump."

Stump smiled. "Keeps me young and on my toes, mate. Just like work keeps me from thinking. I'm gonna tear down the balcony stairs now, and I could sure use some help."

* * *

It was late afternoon before Agent Pearson arrived from Lanai, and like his deceased partner, Holly wouldn't have had a clue about him, either. Portly, unkempt, and gruff, he looked more like a mobster than a fed, and he certainly wasn't out to make any new friends. Fact one: he had a friend who owned a house near Lahaina, and the agents would be taking up residency there. Fact two: he didn't seem to care if Logan was a semiretired DEA agent, or if he was the man on the moon for that matter. Logan's services weren't required, period. Fact three: he wanted everything Al had on the case so far, including the diamonds. Fact four: although somebody else would be sent to handle the body, which would include shipping it back to the mainland, he wanted Morgan's personal effects. And most important was fact five: he didn't need the Lahaina cops breathing down his neck, either, and ordered them all to back off. It was a strange statement because most law enforcement agencies appreciated all the help they could get. But then, Bud Pearson was a strange man. So much so, that by the time he'd finished issuing orders and left with Al, everybody felt relieved to be out of it. Until later that evening, after they'd eaten a makeshift supper, and were sitting around the bar with glum expressions and dark thoughts. The cops had been taken off surveillance duty across the alley and out front, Tutu had gone to Tonoa's sister's house, and Lila had gone home to her kids, so it was just the five of them. Five minds working together, but Logan finally said it best. "To use one of Holly's favorite expressions, something isn't sitting well, but I'll be darned if I know what it is."

Holly had written down all her thoughts on a paper napkin, and finally handed it over to Logan. "If you can get around the squiggles, doodles, and iced tea stains, read this and tell me what you think."

Logan read it, and frowned. "I don't know, sweetheart. That's pretty heavy stuff. I know cops can go bad, but . . ."

Cindy sucked in her cheeks. "Yikes! You think Agent Pearson is a rogue cop?"

"It's a possibility," Holly murmured.

Logan said, "Actually, Holly is suggesting more than that, like maybe Morgan was a bad cop, too. She also thinks there is a third player. The killer who was either working with them and defected, or who has been after them, like they've been after Anita and Brent."

Trying to ignore the disbelief she could see in everybody's eyes, Holly said quickly, "Pearson couldn't be the killer because he was on Lanai at the time, so if it wasn't Anita's brother . . . I know it sounds farfetched, but . . ." She broke off, and gave Logan an imploring glance. "Couldn't you have Pearson and Morgan checked out? I mean, you have so many friends who are Federal agents. Surely it wouldn't take much more than a phone call."

"I suppose I could call in a favor or two," Logan replied.

"Then do it," Holly urged, "and put my mind at ease."

Stump popped the top on a beer can, and took a deep swallow. "I don't see how proving your point would put your mind at ease, Holly. If Pearson turns out to be one of the bad guys, that means he's going to get everything Al has on the case, if he hasn't already. It also means he'll be out there somewhere, watching and waiting, and that's one scary thought. Even worse than that, we don't know what he'll be watching and waiting for."

"Did Al say where Pearson was staying on Lanai?" Danny asked.

Logan picked up the phone off the bar. "No, but I'll ask him."

A few minutes later, Logan was on the line with Al. And although they could only hear Logan's end of the conversation, it wasn't difficult to put it together. Al had turned over Morgan's personal effects, along with everything he had on the case, to Pearson, including the bullets and the report from Ballistics. And no, he had no idea where Pearson had been staying on Lanai. He'd placed the call, and Pearson answered the phone. The only thing he could be sure of was that he had called Lanai.

Holly tugged at Logan's shirtsleeve. "Ask him if he saw any boxes when he went through Morgan's room."

Logan asked, and shook his head.

"What about the phone company? Can't he put a tracer on the number on Lanai?"

Logan asked, and nodded. He winked at Holly, and said into the receiver, "I know. She had 'that feeling' about him right from the beginning. Uh-huh, I know. She should've been a cop. By the way, were the bullets a match?"

Holly could tell by Logan's expression they weren't, and it wasn't a surprise.

Logan hung up, and shrugged. "I don't think I made his day. Meanwhile..." He picked up the phone, and took a deep breath. A few minutes later, he was on the line with one of his DEA buddies in San Francisco.

One hour later, the return call came in from San Francisco. And when Logan finally hung up, his voice quavered with emotion. "Bud Pearson and Richard Morgan, the two agents assigned to the diamond heist, were found dead in a seedy Los Angeles hotel room three weeks ago. Up until now, the agency hasn't had a clue as to the identity of the killer." Logan sat down, and ran a hand through his hair. "It looks like we're going to be overrun with agents after all." Big sigh. "I'd better call Al, and tell him the case of the decade just landed in our laps."

Chapter Eight

Ironically, one of the legitimate agents had a friend who owned a house near Lahaina, and the command post was set up there, leaving everybody at the bar feeling left out, even though they were told they were very much a part of it. Logan had a direct line to the house, which helped, and Tutu had offered her services as their cook, which had been accepted, putting Tonoa into a pan-throwing blue funk because the love of his life was a mile away.

Tonoa's behavior initiated a roundtable discussion late the following morning, and it was quickly decided Holly was the one to set him straight. If he put up this kind of a fuss now,

127

with Tutu only a mile away, what was going
to happen when their vacation, if it could still
be called a vacation, came to an end and they
sailed for Kauai?

Holly found Tonoa in the kitchen chopping
vegetables, and tried to approach the subject
gently. "I know you care a great deal for Tutu,
but her home is on Kauai. She has a job with
us as long as she wants it, and she's a part of
our family. Soon, our vacation will come to an
end, and—"

Tonoa interrupted, and his tone was clipped
and decisive. "Tutu will stay on Maui. *Aloha
nui loa*, much love, yeah. Marry, *hau'oli*, live
in Tonoa's *hale*. Fo' real."

With mixed emotions, not wanting to lose
Tutu, but not wanting to stand in the way of
true love, either, Holly asked, "Have you
talked to Tutu about marriage?"

Tonoa's fat cheeks puffed up, and his dark
eyes snapped. "Fo' what? Tutu knows how I
feel."

Aware he was getting angry again, and nothing would be accomplished by pushing him,
Holly went back to the veranda where the
mood was already glum. They were all there,

with the exception of Lila, who had a meeting with one of her daughter's teachers.

Holly sat down beside Logan, and sighed. "He wants to marry Tutu and keep her here."

"Has he talked to Tutu about it?" Logan asked.

"No, and I'm not sure he's going to. He seems to think Tutu knows how he feels, and she'll do what he wants."

Cindy rolled her eyes. "Wonderful. A Samoan chauvinist."

"I didn't press him," Holly went on, "because I think we should talk to Tutu first."

Logan squeezed Holly's hand. "If Tutu wants to stay, we can't stop her."

Holly sighed again. "I know. But I can't help but wonder if she's getting the real picture here."

Danny poured coffee into a cup from the silver carafe on the table, and dumped in a spoonful of sugar. "I'm afraid the same thing could be said for us. So Logan has a direct line to the command post, and we've been told we're part of the team. It's almost noon, and we haven't heard word one. Makes me think they've been stroking us to keep us pacified, and have no intentions of using our services." He looked at

Logan. ''Well? Come on, Logan. You've been an agent for a long time. Give us your take on this.''

''Unfortunately, you're probably right,'' Logan said. ''My affiliation has always been with the DEA, you understand, but I would suppose most Federal agencies work the same way. Outside help isn't necessarily reliable, and therefore it's rarely used. I think the direct phone line was put in solely for their benefit if, in fact, we happen to stumble onto something important, and Tutu is at the command post because they needed a cook who liked cops, and who could handle an assortment of appetites around the clock. That's it.''

''That's it?'' Holly said incredulously. ''I can't believe you're willing to sit back and do nothing.''

Logan gave her a sly grin. ''Who said I'm going to sit back and look the other way? I think it's time to put Plan A into motion.''

Holly raised a brow. ''Plan A?''

''Uh-huh, and after that, we'll go to Plan B, if necessary.''

''Translation?''

''It's simple enough. Plan A deals with the facts. Plan B has to do with our gut instincts.

"Okay, since Anita's death, I've been keeping track of the facts." He pointed at the notebook on the table. "I've listed most of them, along with some of my thoughts."

Stump pointed at his head. "My list is up here."

Logan smiled. "Sometimes, that's the best way. Then you can't lose it." He opened the notebook. "Shall we start with the facts? Last night, Agent Holt told us that the list of days and times Holly found taped behind the painting were the days and times of the various diamond heists on the mainland. What doesn't figure is why Anita thought the list was important enough to hide. Who was she hiding it from, and why? The question mark is pretty big after that one.

"We also know Anita and the man who called himself Ric Brown—and I'll refer to him as Ric because we don't have his real name—were both shot with bullets from a nine-millimeter handgun, but the bullets weren't a match. Anita was found in the water near the wharf, wrapped up in a painter's drop cloth. Death occurred sometime after midnight. Other than Brent, Holly and I were the last people to see her alive. That was a little after eleven the night before, when we saw her talking to Brent in the alley behind the bar. At that point in time, we didn't know they were brother and sister.

''Ric wasn't found in the water, but near the wharf. Nobody heard anything, or saw anything, so we can assume the killer used a silencer. We know the killer wasn't Ric's partner, because he was on Lanai at the time. We now know where he was staying, and that he had a private phone in his room. We also know before he made the trip to Maui, he paid the bill in full with cash, and wiped the room clean, which tells me he wasn't planning on going back to Lanai.''

''And we know brother Brent is still missing,'' Danny added.

Stump sighed. ''It's beginning to sound more and more like 'brother Brent' is the killer.''

Logan nodded. ''Well, we sure can't count him out.''

Holly was doodling on a paper napkin, and made a smiley face with a droopy mouth. ''We know Ric was carrying Agent Morgan's identification, so I think we can assume the bad guy who came over from Lanai was carrying Agent

Pearson's ID. Which means they took the real agents' identification after they killed them. They knew using the agents' identities would open all kinds of doors, and basically, it did.''

Danny said, ''I think we can assume 'Ric Brown' wasn't the dead guy's real name, either.''

Logan jotted down a few notes. ''If his fingerprints are on file, the feds will come up with a name. Meanwhile, be it Brent, or somebody else, the killer is still out there, somewhere.''

Stump asked, ''Do you think the bogus Pearson took off after he got what he wanted from Al?''

''No, I don't,'' Logan said. ''Because he didn't get what he wanted from Al. We've been told the diamonds we found were only a small part of the heist, so it's safe to assume the rest were in the other boxes, stuffed down in the excelsior. Only he doesn't have the boxes. Ric had the boxes. Now Ric is dead, and the boxes are missing.''

''Guess that's a pretty good reason to stick around,'' Stump muttered.

Logan returned, ''That's right. I also think it's safe to say he thinks the rest of the loot is still here in the bar. But back to Ric. He took the boxes, assuming he had all the diamonds. When he found some of them missing, he started a search, beginning with the *Sea Breeze*. I have no doubt in my mind now that he was the man who Danny confronted. Both on board, and in the alley.''

''So why did he attack Danny in the alley?'' Cindy asked.

''I have no idea unless he wanted to send us a message, thinking we might tie in Anita's death with the assault. You know, 'I killed Anita, and I'll kill *you* if you don't back off.'

''In retrospect, it's easy to put the preceding events into focus. Somehow, Ric and his partner found out Anita and her brother had settled on Lanai. They kept them under surveillance, but not so they could move in and make an arrest. They were prepared to kill them, as soon as they had the diamonds. Only before that happened, Anita relocated in Lahaina. The brother followed a short time later. But because brother and sister hadn't given up their room on Lanai, one of the bad guys had to stay behind. Maybe they tossed a coin, and Ric won the toss.

''Al said the bogus Pearson was genuinely upset when he talked to him on the phone.

Well, I can understand that. His partner in crime was dead, and that put a third player on the scene. I think it was at that point in time he had to make a split decision. He had to make the jaunt to Maui as Agent Pearson, and play it out, which would include giving Al all the particulars about the ring of crooks and the diamond heist. He did, and we all know the results. It almost worked. If I hadn't made that call to San Francisco, we'd be sitting here right now, waiting to hear from 'Agent Pearson.' "

Holly gave an involuntary shudder. "We still might hear from him, Logan. He has no way of knowing we're on to him, or that the real feds are here on the island."

Cindy made a face that came out like a grimace. "Has anybody considered the possibility that maybe the killer took the boxes?"

Logan muttered, "Unfortunately, I've considered it. If that's the way it happened, it leaves us with a pretty hefty question. Does the killer know some of the diamonds are missing? If he does, he could be hanging around, too, putting us all at risk. If he doesn't, he could be on the mainland by now, and without a clue to his identity . . ."

"Catching him would be a major undertaking,'' Holly concluded. "Well, no matter who took the boxes, if that person is still in Lahaina and he thinks the missing diamonds are still in the bar, he's in for a surprise if he thinks he's going to get in by way of the alley stairs."

Stump grinned. "All he'll find is a pile of wood in the alley. We'll keep the balcony door and the downstairs back door, along with the front door and windows, padlocked at night, and let him stew."

"We'll take it one step further than that," Logan announced. "We'll take turns keeping watch at night. Two at a time, say five-hour shifts."

"Maybe Al can help us out there," Holly reasoned. "If he can assign an officer to keep watch . . ."

Cindy finally grinned. "Like maybe Pupule Mauna?"

"Well, he certainly is formidable."

Logan looked at his watch. "Al said he'd stop by around two, so I suppose we can ask him then." He winked at Danny. "I think it's about time we met this crazy mountain of a man who has charmed our ladies right out of their senses."

His comment brought chuckles around, and it helped ease the tension.

A few minutes later, Danny cleared his throat. "Um, what do you suppose Anita and her brother were eventually going to do with the diamonds?"

"Find a fence would be my guess," Holly said. "Although I don't think it would have been here in the islands. I think this was just a place to lie low. A year, maybe two."

Stump muttered, "And in the meantime, she would've worked her way back into my heart. Dumb as a stump, that's me."

Holly eyed Stump intently. "You all but said you weren't in love with her, but that she was like a breath of fresh air. If you were simply lonely and looking for female companionship, you really didn't have to look any further than your lovely bartender."

A wide grin broke across Stump's rugged face. "You mean Lila? Yeah, I know. We've done some talking. She told me how she feels. Like I said, dumb as a stump, that's me."

"So how do *you* feel?" Holly asked.

"Flattered, I guess. And yeah, I like her, too. But we agreed to take things slow. Friends first, and then . . ." The gold tooth sparkled in the sunlight. "If it gets beyond friendship, you'll be the first to know.

"Now, I think I'd better check on things in the kitchen. Tonoa is supposed to be fixing vegetable soup for lunch. Better make sure he hasn't spiked it with red pepper or crushed glass, or maybe emptied a bottle of pikake perfume into the broth."

After Stump had gone inside, Holly glanced at Cindy, and her smile faded. "What is it, Cindy? You look like you've seen a ghost."

Cindy groaned. "Worse than that. I've just decided I'm as dumb as a stump, too. When Stump mentioned the pikake perfume.... Well, that day Lila and I packed up Anita's things, I put Anita's purse on top of the highboy, and I don't remember taking it down. It was so high up, I had to sort of toss it, you know? I would've had to climb on a chair to get it down, and it truly slipped my mind."

Logan gave Cindy a comforting smile. "Don't worry about it, Cin. From what I understand, there wasn't much in it anyway, though I suppose we should turn it over to Al." He stood up. "I'll go get it."

Cindy shook her head. "I don't believe I did

that. Guess I was still pretty upset because I saw Anita's body. . . ."

"And understandably so," Holly soothed, but her thoughts were on something else. Anita's room had smelled so strongly of the potent perfume, it had been overpowering. She'd been carrying one of the bottles in her purse, too, when, in fact, Stump had said she didn't wear perfume because she was allergic to it.

"Holly?" Cindy said, frowning with concern. "Now *you're* the one who looks funny."

"I just thought of something. . . ."

At that moment, Logan walked out on the veranda, carrying Anita's purse. The minute he placed it on the table, Holly reached in and took out the bottle of perfume. Seconds later, she dumped the contents into her empty coffee cup, and there, with the eye-burning fumes wafting up, amid the light golden-colored liquid, and under the tiny, artificial orchid that floated on the surface, lay a perfect, dazzling, blue-white diamond.

"Whoa!" Logan exclaimed.

Holly fished out the diamond, and placed it on the dark wood table where it would catch the rays of the sun. It was exquisitely beautiful, but hosted a whole new set of questions, and problems. "This explains the smell of perfume in Anita's room," she said finally. "She probably spilled some of it when she dropped in the diamond. It also looks like she was holding out on her brother."

Logan's response was quick and succinct. "Well, if she was and he wasn't the loving brother, I'd say we're looking at a motive for murder."

Chapter Nine

Double crosses and triple crosses seemed to be the name of the game. Anita and Brent had double crossed the big boys, and now it looked as though Anita had double crossed her brother, which would also account for her keeping the times and dates taped to the back of the painting. If she got caught, she could blow the whistle on everyone. And not to be overlooked was the fact that if Al Gainer hadn't told the bogus Agent Pearson about the small cache of diamonds they'd found in the box with the pikake perfume, the man wouldn't have known his partner had taken the boxes in the first place, meaning "Ric" hadn't bothered

141

to call him on Lanai and tell him. But then there was also the fact that maybe Ric hadn't taken the boxes, somebody else was the culprit, and that person had hoodwinked them all.

By the time Al arrived at two, Holly had the clawing kind of headache that made her hair hurt, and worse, Tonoa had gone home in a snit, nearly demolishing the kitchen in the process.

"That's it!" Stump exclaimed. "He goes out with the dishwater in the morning. Anita might have had an ulterior motive for wanting me to fire him, but right now, my reasons seem more than valid. He's become a hazard to my establishment, and I don't care if he's in love with Tutu, or Madam Pele herself!"

Lila had arrived just before the ruckus, and gave Stump a comforting hug. "I know where he lives. Do you want me to go talk to him? Maybe I can settle him down."

"Settle him down until what, the next time? The only person he seems to listen to lately is Tutu, and she's at the command post, cooking for the agents. That's part of the problem, you know. He resents the fact she's over there with a bunch of men."

"Maybe he's jealous," Lila reasoned.

"Maybe, and maybe my patience has finally reached the end of its rope. I've been putting up with his shenanigans for years, and I've tried to be understanding. But enough is enough!"

After Lila followed Stump into the bar, Al shook his head. "Every place I've gone today, I've found people with attitude problems. And that includes the command post. Tempers are short to say the least, and when I left, Tutu was threatening to walk out on them."

"So, they can't get the case to come together, huh?" Logan said, giving Al a sly smile. "Maybe they should talk to us." He handed Al the diamond, and explained.

Al rolled it over in his hand, and sighed. "I know you're upset because you feel left out of things, but this looks like pretty important evidence to me. You should've called the command post, Logan."

Logan heaved a weary sigh. "I did, but I couldn't get to first base. I talked to an Agent Grecho, and he all but hung up on me."

"Did you tell him you found a diamond?"

"I didn't want to put that kind of information out over the phone lines, but I made sure

he understood we'd found some important evidence.''

"Didn't wash, huh?"

"No, it didn't. I even said I'd deliver it, but
that was nixed, too. So, now the diamond is all
yours. At least they'll let *you* through the door.
Meanwhile, I'm not about to sit around like the
nerdy DEA agent they seem to take me for.
Holly and I are going to spend the rest of the
day on the wharf, poking around. We have to
clean things up on the *Sea Breeze* anyway, and
this seems like a good time to do it.''

"Want me to get an officer to assist you?"
Al asked.

"No, but you can assign an officer to help
guard the bar tonight. All night, if it's possible.''

"Somebody like Sergeant Joe Kaloni would
certainly be an asset,'' Cindy said, smiling up
at him.

Al nodded. "Consider it done." He looked
down at the diamond in his hand. "Guess I'd
better get this over to the command post, and
see what they say. Don't suppose it will bring
on a round of smiles.''

Holly spoke up, and her voice was tight.

"What are they doing, Al? Or are they doing anything?"

"Not much that I could see. When I walked in, Agent Grecho was setting out grids, but all that came to a screeching halt when he saw me. I wanted to remind him I'm not the enemy, this is my town, my island, and I might be able to help, but by the look on his face, I thought I'd better keep my opinions to myself."

"How many agents are we talking about?" Logan asked.

"Holt, Grecho, and two young men who look like rookies. All from Oahu. The team still hasn't arrived from the mainland."

"Then you'd better get the diamond to the command post before they arrive, or you might not be able to get through the door."

A few minutes later, Holly and Logan headed for the wharf, but it wasn't until they were on the *Sea Breeze* that Holly finally spoke her mind. "I think the whole thing stinks, Logan. We have an unidentified killer running loose, a man on the loose who is without a doubt a mobster and a killer, missing diamonds, and a bunch of Federal agents who apparently haven't a foggy clue as to what they're doing."

Logan picked up a box of papers that had been overturned on the salon floor, and sighed. ''I understand your frustration, sweetheart, because I feel it, too.''

Holly returned the cushions to the built-in couch, and fluffed up the loose pillows. ''Assuming Ric was responsible for making this mess and assaulting Danny, how did he know the *Sea Breeze* was connected to Stump's bar?''

''Did you mention the *Sea Breeze* when you talked to him?''

''No, I didn't. The second time I talked to him, I told him we lived on a neighboring island, so he might have assumed we sailed over, but that was after the assault on Danny.''

''Maybe Stump told him.''

''Maybe, but I doubt it. . . . You know, it wouldn't have taken much for Ric to remove the diamonds from the boxes and then dispose of the boxes in a Dumpster.''

''So what did he do with the diamonds?'' Logan asked, eyeing Holly intently, like her answer was all-important.

She gave him a wan smile. ''Are you asking me to give you my gut instinct?''

"Only because your gut instinct is usually right on."

"Okay, then try this. Supposedly, the rest of the diamonds would easily fit into an eight-by-ten manila envelope, or something of equal size. In other words, the diamonds would be easy to carry around without drawing attention. What if the real reason Ric assaulted Danny in the alley was to stall for time? What if he wasn't looking for the missing diamonds on the *Sea Breeze* at all, but was stashing the ones he had instead. What if this mess in the salon was created because he was looking for a spot to hide them? I mean, there really isn't much clutter. A couple of overturned boxes, cushions off the sofa. He was probably going to set everything right before he went ashore.

"Okay, so Danny interrupted him, and he took off, with Danny in pursuit. What if he assaulted Danny in the alley, and then came back to the *Sea Breeze*? You following me so far?"

Logan nodded. "I'm ahead of you, sweetheart. What if the killer killed Ric because he thought Ric had the diamonds on him? Only he didn't because he had already stashed them on board the *Sea Breeze*?"

Holly shook her head. "Then we should be looking for the diamonds instead of cleaning things up. But you know, that's the part that doesn't fit. And it goes right back to my original question. How did Ric know the *Sea Breeze* was connected to Stump's bar? And more important, even if he knew it and that we were the owners, why would he chance stashing the diamonds on board when we could sail away in a heartbeat?"

"Or find the diamonds," Logan added. "Well, it was a thought. I think we have to assume he was looking for the diamonds. Now all we have to do is figure out how he knew about the *Sea Breeze*."

"Brent knew," Holly offered. "Maybe when some of the diamonds turned up missing, he thought about the boat right off."

"That would mean Brent and Ric were working together."

Holly sighed. "Maybe Brent and Ric had their heads together to bamboozle 'Pearson,' and then Brent turned on Ric and killed him."

"Which means there is a very good possibility Brent has the missing diamonds, and he's many miles away by now."

Holly sat down at a corner table, and ran a

hand through her hair. "You're leaving out the good part, my love. If it was a double cross, I'll bet my left big toe the bogus Pearson isn't aware of it."

"But he knows somebody killed his partner, so that means he's looking over his shoulder, just like we are."

"It also makes me wonder how Anita fit in. Do you still have the photo of Anita and Brent?"

"I do." He pointed at the notebook he'd placed on the table. "It's in the back."

"Well, maybe we should show it around Lahaina and the neighboring areas. When Al was trying to find Brent, he just asked questions because he didn't have the photo at that time. I know there is a good chance Brent is long gone, but what if he isn't? And what if we're wrong? What if he isn't the killer, and he's gone into hiding?"

Logan's dark eyes flickered with uneasiness. "I'd say that's a pretty scary scenario, sweetheart. Because if what you say is true, and he wasn't working with Ric, that means we still have an unidentified third party who knew about the *Sea Breeze*, and could very well be the killer."

Holly shivered. "I was thinking it; I just didn't want to say it."

Logan reached over and picked up the notebook. "So, what do you say we show the photo around the wharf and then work our way toward town?"

Holly nodded, and followed Logan out on deck. She didn't really believe they were going to find Brent, but for their own peace of mind, they had to try.

The slip to the right of the *Sea Breeze* was still empty, and to the left, the yacht called *Sweet Alice* still sat in silent repose. Beyond, a man was sitting on the deck of the party boat, and although he pretended to be reading some sort of a newspaper, Holly could feel his watchful eyes. "Let's start with the man on the party boat," she said, slipping an arm around Logan's waist.

"He's been watching us," Logan said, trying to keep his voice casual.

But Holly caught the tone. There was an edge to it, one she'd heard many times before. Usually when he sensed danger. She could feel the bulge of his gun under his bright aloha shirt, and took a deep breath.

"Aloha," the man said, when Holly and Logan walked up the gangplank. "Beautiful afternoon."

He was short, portly, and his smile didn't reach his eyes. He was wearing shorts and an unbuttoned aloha shirt, displaying a massive chest.

"Beautiful afternoon," Holly returned, shaking his hand. "My name is Holly, and this is my husband, Logan. We own the cruiser over there. . . ."

He shook Logan's hand and nodded. "Uh-huh. The *Sea Breeze*. She's a beauty. The name is Turner. Ted Turner. Ha ha ha. No, I'm not *the* Ted Turner. Just call me Mr. T. Everybody does. You want a drink? Coffee? Maybe a soda?"

"No thanks," Logan said, handing Mr. T. the photo. "We're trying to locate the man in the photo. Have you seen him?"

Ted Turner studied the photo, and frowned. "I haven't seen the man, but I've seen the lady. Real looker."

"And where was that?" Holly asked.

His eyes narrowed. "You two cops?"

"We're just friends," Holly assured him.

"Hmm, well, guess it's been a few days

since I've seen her. Hmm. Maybe two or three.''

Logan asked, ''Can you tell us where you saw her?''

''Down here on the wharf.''

Holly exchanged glances with Logan before she said, ''Do you know who owns the *Sweet Alice*?''

''Can't say I do. A big dude, and he isn't exactly the friendly type. He sailed in a couple of weeks ago. I wanted to be neighborly, so I invited him to one of my parties. You'd think I'd driven a stake through his heart.''

''Can you describe him?'' Holly asked.

''Not really.''

''Is he staying on the boat?'' Logan asked.

''Don't think so. Sorry I can't be more help.''

A few minutes later, in a little park that fronted the far end of the wharf, Holly and Logan sat down on a bench and both spoke at once.

Logan gave her a hug. ''I know. Great minds work together. Mr. T was pretty evasive. Too evasive. He invited the owner of the *Sweet Alice* to one of his parties, and yet he couldn't describe him.''

"But he said the *Sweet Alice* sailed in a couple of weeks ago, Logan. What if the man he couldn't describe was Ric? It sure fits, because that's about the same time Ric walked into the bar and asked for a job. It also might explain how Ric knew about the *Sea Breeze*. He could have seen us that day we sailed in."

"When Stump and Anita met us on the wharf," Logan added. "It would explain the assault on Danny, too. When Danny and I sailed back from Lanai, he could've been on board the *Sweet Alice*, and saw me leave."

"And if he didn't know Danny was on board . . ." Holly shook her head. "At that point in time, he'd already taken the boxes out of Anita's room, realized some of the diamonds were missing, but realized, too, that somebody at the bar had packed Anita's things, and that person could very well have the rest of the diamonds. The *Sea Breeze* would have been a logical place to begin the search."

Logan frowned. "But what about Anita? How did she fit in? We know 'Pearson' and 'Ric' had the brother and sister under surveillance, and were planning to kill them as soon as they had the diamonds."

"It might have been totally innocent on her

part," Holly reasoned. "She had no idea who Ric was. He came into the bar that day, looking for a job, and she was smitten. Don't forget, she was the one who was after Stump to hire him."

"And she was the one who suggested Stump put in stairs from the balcony to the alley because she liked to take late-night walks, and wanted easier outside access. Now all we have to do is fit Brent in, and we'll have the perfect triangle."

"If we can fit Brent in, we'll have the killer," Holly said, leaning her head against Logan's shoulder. "It's nice here. The view is spectacular and the air is filled with the sweet scent of frangipane. I can almost forget we're in the middle of a murder case, when we're supposed to be celebrating our first anniversary."

Logan kissed her softly. "Then I suggest we solve the case so we still have time to do all those things we were planning to do."

"Mmm, like take moonlit walks along the beach?"

"Uh-huh, and drift to sleep in each other's arms to the sound of the pounding surf."

"Sounds pretty spectacular, Mr. West."

"It sounds spectacular, and wonderful. . . . Holly?"

Holly took a deep, grating breath. "A thought just occurred to me. The bogus Agent Pearson has to know about the *Sweet Alice*."

Logan puffed out his cheeks. "Say no more."

"We should tell the agents. . . ."

Logan shook his head. "From the way they've been described, I sincerely believe they would botch the whole thing."

"Then we should at least tell Al."

"That's the plan. I'll go talk to him now. Hopefully, he's back in his office."

She was looking at him, and he could read her thoughts. "You want to stay on board the *Sea Breeze* and keep an eye on the *Sweet Alice*, right? No way, Holly. It's too dangerous. I can't let you do that."

"I think it would be a good idea. You wouldn't be gone long. And I have Pearl."

Holly was referring to the pearl-handled .38 she always carried. She grinned and patted her tote. "She's right here, and she's loaded."

Logan kissed the tip of her nose, and sighed. "There's no use arguing with you, so let's get you settled on board so I can be on my way."

"No . . . Just go, Logan. The sooner you get this information to Al, the better."

"Okay, but promise you'll take care?"

"I promise. . . ."

Holly watched Logan until he was out of sight, and then headed for the boat, feeling the kind of excitement she always felt when they were close to solving a case. She had no doubt in her mind that the phony Agent Pearson was hiding out on the *Sweet Alice,* and in a very short time, he would be behind bars.

Chapter Ten

Ted Turner was no longer on the deck of his boat when Holly boarded the *Sea Breeze,* and it was just as well. His watchful wariness had been disconcerting to say the least, and it was always better to observe than be observed.

For the next hour, Holly finished straightening up the salon, but kept an eye on the *Sweet Alice* through the portholes. Not that she expected ''Pearson'' to appear on deck until he had the cover of darkness, and admittedly, the thought of him slinking around at night, keeping his own watchful vigil, was a chilling one.

Wondering if Al would use the Harbor Patrol as backup before the police moved in,

Holly was in the small galley and had just put water on for tea, when she heard movement behind her. Thinking it was Logan, she smiled.

But before she could turn around, a deep voice said, "Stand perfectly still, Mrs. West. I have a gun, and it's aimed at your back."

Holly didn't recognize the voice, so it wasn't Pearson. Brent? It had to be, so she challenged his arrival with, "You won't get away with this, Brent."

Amusement frosted his voice. "So you know who I am. Anita said you were a P.I., so maybe that's what makes you so smart."

It was a snide remark, and Holly's response was brusque. "I'm smart enough to know all about you, Brent. Have you been following me?"

His answer was almost a snicker. "How else would I know you were alone?"

"Sounds like you're pretty smart, too."

"Smart enough," came his quick reply.

"Then you shouldn't have any problem answering my question. Did you kill your sister?"

"Is that what the cops think?" he asked.

His tone had changed; the arrogance was gone. Holly took a deep breath, and turned around. Wanting to hate the man, but feeling only pity because of the pain she could see in his eyes, she repeated, ''Did you kill your sister?''

Anger replaced the pain. ''Ric Brown killed her. That day he walked into the bar looking for a job, she fell in love. I tried to tell her you don't fall in love just like that. She wouldn't listen.''

''Is that what you were discussing the night my husband and I saw you in the alley behind the bar? The night Anita was killed?''

His eyes narrowed over her. ''Yeah, well, we were in the alley that night, but we sure didn't see you.''

''That's because we didn't want you to. That was also the night you disappeared, Brent, making you the prime suspect.''

Holly's gun was in her tote, and the tote was on the breakfast-nook table. She took a few calculated steps. The gun Brent was holding wasn't the murder weapon. It was a revolver with a rusty barrel, and his finger wasn't on the trigger. At that moment, she knew he hadn't killed Ric, either. It was a disturbing thought, because that meant there was a third player after all. But she found the thought comforting, too, because at least she wasn't at the mercy of a killer.

"I had to disappear," he said finally. "Otherwise, I'd be dead, too." He waved the gun around. "You know how to run this tug?"

His description of the *Sea Breeze* brought a smile to her face. "My husband is the sailor. I don't know the difference between fore and aft. But even if I did, and your idea here is to make your escape on the *Sea Breeze*, we wouldn't get out of the harbor. The Harbor Patrol has been alerted, and they have orders to check all outgoing traffic."

Wondering if he'd bought her lie, she took another step. "You look terrible, Brent. Why don't you sit down while I fix you a cup of tea, and then we can talk about it."

His shoulders slumped. "Talk about what? The fact that my sister is dead? The fact that I'm wanted by the police? The fact that Ric is out there somewhere, waiting to kill me, too?"

"Ric Brown is dead," Holly said matter-of-factly. "He was shot at close range, and his body was found near the wharf. Now, would you like to sit down?"

Brent dropped to a padded seat at the table,

and ran a hand over his eyes. "I-I didn't know...."

Holly was standing close to him now, and reached out. "I didn't think you did. Give me the gun, Brent, and then we can talk." He handed her the gun, and after a quick check, she shook her head. "Where did you get this piece of junk? The cylinder is jammed, and the firing pin is gone."

"I got it from a guy in a waterfront bar for ten bucks right after I got to Lahaina. I knew it wouldn't shoot, but I still felt better carrying it."

Wanting to tell him it was a good way to get killed, too, she let it go. "You'll feel better if you come clean, too, and give yourself up to the authorities. As it stands now, you're wanted in connection with a string of diamond heists on the mainland. Small potatoes compared to murder."

"I'm not a killer," he said dejectedly.

"Maybe not, but the police don't know that. As we speak, Federal agents are storming the island."

"That doesn't sound like small potatoes to me."

"They aren't after you. They're after a couple of cop killers, though I don't suppose they would mind taking you into custody.'' Holly explained while she fixed two cups of tea, and then waited for the reaction she hoped would come. He didn't disappoint her.

Brent's face turned pale. "Then those two hoods were planning to kill us all along."

The fact that he'd referred to the bogus agents as "hoods" when he, in fact, had been a member of a gang of diamond thieves, brought another smile to her face. But the humor was short-lived as she considered their plight. Arresting Brent might close one chapter, but there was still a killer at large.

Holly sat down at the table, encouraged Brent to drink the tea, and waited. He wanted to talk, and she was willing to listen, though she still kept an eye on the *Sweet Alice*.

Brent took a sip of tea, and wiped his mouth with the back of his hand. "I was the one who turned Anita on to the diamonds. She was down on her luck at the time, and I was making good money. It was the first time she'd ever done anything illegal, but you know the old saying—money talks."

"We know all about the operation," Holly said, "and the fact the two of you decided to keep the diamonds you were carrying from the last heist for yourselves.'' She almost told him about the lone diamond in the bottle of pikake perfume, but what would be the point now? Anita was dead.

''Yeah, well, we planned to hide out in the islands for a while, and eventually go back to the mainland.''

''Were you hoping to be able to fence the diamonds in the islands?''

Brent shrugged. ''We talked about it, but we didn't know where to begin. Our contacts were all on the mainland. I suppose eventually we would've found somebody.''

''What happened that night Anita was killed?'' Holly asked. ''Were you a witness to the murder?''

His jaw tightened, and tears filled his eyes. ''That night you saw us in the alley, well, Anita was planning to meet Ric near the wharf. I was trying to talk her out of it.''

''Is that why she had Stump build the steps from the balcony to the alley? So she could come and go as she pleased?''

''Yeah, that's why, and Stump swallowed her story about being an insomniac. Guess he thought he was in love, too. Anyway, I'd seen her with Ric a couple of times before that night, and I didn't like the way he treated her. But I couldn't talk her out of it, so I followed her to the wharf. It was late, and nobody was around. I stayed in the shadows. I could tell something was wrong right off. And then he started slapping her around. Everything gets pretty fuzzy after that, but I remember running up to them and brandishing my gun. My only thought at that time was to get her out of harm's way. He pulled a gun and aimed it at me. Anita cried out and jumped in front of me just as he pulled the trigger. Anita took the bullet intended for me. . . ."

Tears were flowing freely down his cheeks, and he didn't bother to wipe them away. "Don't ask me how, but I knew she was dead. I went a little crazy, I guess, and charged him. He fell back and hit his head on a piling. That's when I took off. He wasn't dead, just stunned, and it didn't take much to figure out I'd be next, if he could find me."

"Where have you been staying?" Holly asked, feeling nothing but sympathy for this man who had chosen the wrong path to follow, and who obviously felt responsible for his sister's death.

"Mostly around the wharf, though I think I've managed to find every abandoned building and back alleyway in Lahaina. I haven't had a shower since the night Anita was killed, and I'm wearing the same clothes. I had to leave everything I own behind."

"In the room you were renting on Lanai?"

"Some of it. The rest of it is in an old abandoned fisherman's shack down the beach. You know about Lanai, huh?"

"We know, and we know the bad guys had a room close by and were watching you. The fact that the two of you got this far is remarkable. They could have taken you out at any time."

Brent was shivering, and tears filled his eyes again. "Maybe it would've been better that way. Then I wouldn't be doing all this mental suffering. Anita was the only family I had. The old man walked out on us when we were kids, and our mama died before I turned thirteen. Protective Services tried to take over after that, but we stayed one step ahead of them. Anita and me, well, we sort of went our separate ways after that. She was sixteen and went to live with some friends. I looked eighteen, and got a job in a warehouse. I slept on the streets until I had enough money to get a room. I tried to get Anita to move in with me, but she had big plans. A few months after that, she left California for Florida. We kept in touch, but I didn't see her for quite a few years. Then one day, she returned to L.A. By that time, she was down on her luck, and I was working for John Lewis. He was a businessman by day, and a jewel thief by night.''

Holly said, ''The name John Lewis isn't familiar to me, but as I understand it, the authorities busted the diamond ring two months ago.''

''Yeah, and it was all a matter of timing. After a heist, we always met John at a designated place. That's when he would give us the diamonds and our instructions.''

''Us. You and Anita? Or all the players?''

''All the players. That night, Anita wasn't feeling well, and we got there early. John gave us the diamonds, and we left. Later that night, we heard about the bust, and that's when we decided to keep the diamonds.''

''Somebody had to know you hadn't been arrested, and still had the diamonds, Brent. Any idea who that was?''

Brent shrugged. "John's brother, maybe. He was there that night, and knew we left early."

"Do you know if he was arrested?"

"I didn't see his name in the paper."

"What was his name?"

"Martin Lewis."

"Can you describe him?" Holly asked.

Brent shrugged again. "Middle-aged. Heavy. Dark hair. Mean."

"You've just described 'Pearson,' Brent."

Brent shuddered. "The brother wasn't a part of John's operation, but with John in jail, John probably asked Martin to clean up the loose ends."

Holly sighed. "And I'm sure John considered you and your sister very big loose ends."

"More than likely. The diamonds we were carrying were worth a couple of million. One diamond in particular was worth a lot."

The diamond Anita had stashed in the pikake perfume.

Holly added fresh tea bags to their cups, and filled the cups with hot water. She needed a few moments to sort it out in her mind, because there were simply too many players. Finally, she said, "Help me with this, Brent. John Lewis and his gang, with the exception of you and your sister, are in jail. Martin Lewis wasn't a part of the operation, but he could be helping his brother. The man we know as Ric worked with Martin. They were on Lanai together, and had you under surveillance. We know Martin couldn't have killed Ric, so who did?''

Brent added a packet of Sweet 'n Low to his tea, and grimaced. ''Well, whoever it was, has the diamonds.''

''But maybe he didn't get all of them,'' Holly offered. ''Remember, Detective Gainer turned the diamonds we found over to the bogus Pearson, believing he was a Federal agent. I think we have two separate factions here, Brent. Martin Lewis and Ric killed the two agents and took their identification. From that point on, they became Agents Bud Pearson and Richard Morgan. It opened doors for them, and they took advantage of it. They followed you to Lanai, and kept you under surveillance. Then Anita left for Maui. The partner, the man we know as Ric, followed her. A short time later, you made the trip to Maui, but you didn't give up your room. Martin figured you were coming back, so stayed on Lanai. I told you what happened after that.

''Okay, so Detective Gainer turned the diamonds we found over to Martin Lewis, believing he was an agent. . . ."

"So maybe whoever killed Martin's partner, or Ric Brown, has the rest of them."

"But that isn't the whole story, Brent. No matter whether we're dealing with one faction or two, one particular stone has been left out of the equation."

"The diamond I was telling you about?"

"That's right. And your sister had it. I found it in a bottle of pikake perfume. The feds have it now."

A flurry of emotions played across Brent's face, ending with a curious kind of admiration. "Looks like I was a good teacher, and Anita was a pretty fast learner. So, if each side thinks the other side has that particular diamond . . ."

"That's why they are still on the island." Holly looked out at the *Sweet Alice*. Late-afternoon sunlight was glinting against the portholes, like diamonds. It had been a long time since Logan had gone in search of Al. It would be dark soon, and under the cover of darkness, anything could happen. If Ric knew about the *Sea Breeze*, Martin Lewis probably knew about it, too. It was something they should have considered.

She weighed the possibilities, and looked at Brent. "You're carrying around a gun that won't fire, but if it was operable, could you shoot it?"

A slight smile tugged at the corners of his mouth. "I was given a crash course in weaponry when I went to work for Lewis. Yeah, I could shoot it."

Holly took a key ring out of her tote, and stood up. There was a small locked storage area under the padded seat, which contained an assortment of weapons. She unlocked it, and extracted a nine-millimeter Beretta. "Think you could handle this?" she asked, placing the gun on the table.

He stared at the gun, and then stared at her. "You'd trust me with that?"

"I'm a pretty good judge of character, and you aren't a killer. I guess what I'm saying is, if you want to take the gun and run, you'll have to kill me first." She took the .38 out of her tote and smiled. "Provided I don't shoot you first. We have a dilemma here, Brent, and I have to make a decision. We think Pearson— Martin Lewis—is hiding on the *Sweet Alice*." She pointed out the porthole.

Brent's face bleached white. "Right there in the next slip?"

"Yes, and my husband has gone to notify Detective Gainer." Holly bit her lip. "He's been gone a long time. Too long. I'm scared to death something has happened, but I can't leave. I'm supposed to be keeping an eye on the boat so Lewis doesn't get away. Can't call, either, because we don't have a phone on board."

Brent hunkered over, and held his arms to his chest. "Man, so use the radio and call the Harbor Patrol, or something."

"The boat has to be running to use the radio, and my husband has the keys."

He looked at her incredulously. "Then you want me to stay here and keep watch while you track him down?"

"That's one of the possibilities."

"Man, do I want to hear the other one?"

"If you'll help me, we might be able to take him by surprise."

Brent sighed. "That's what I was afraid you were gonna say."

"I can't guarantee anything, but it might help your case with the authorities."

Brent made a face and shrugged. "If I'm dead, my case is closed."

"But we'll have the element of surprise," Holly coaxed, "and it would be two guns against one."

Brent frowned. "He could have an arsenal over there."

"But he's only one man with two hands. Once we have him neutralized, he's bound to have the keys to the boat. We can use the radio then to call for help, and . . ."

Amusement finally replaced the anxiety in his eyes. "You've got this all figured out, haven't you?"

"Well, not exactly, but if we don't do something, I truly believe one of two things will happen as soon as it gets dark. Either he's going to sneak on board the *Sea Breeze* and take us by surprise, or he'll get away. Oh, I know. The Harbor Patrol might eventually catch up with him, but under the cover of darkness, he could also get away."

Brent heaved a sigh. "So, do we wait for the cover of darkness to sneak on board?"

"Nope. We'll do it right now, so we'll have the protection of daylight. I know that probably sounds strange, but if we run into trouble, we'll have a better chance of being seen or heard.''

''So, I suppose you want to do this now?''

''Right now, though I want to leave my husband a note.''

After she wrote the note, Brent followed Holly out on deck, and his apprehension matched her own, even though there were people strolling along the wharf.

The *Sea Breeze* and the *Sweet Alice* shared a small section of dock that ran between the two boats. Holly couldn't see the party boat from where they were standing, but that also meant Ted Turner couldn't see them. It was just as well, because she had no idea how he would react if he saw them sneaking on board.

''Now what?'' Brent asked, looking up at the *Sweet Alice.*

''We climb the gangplank quietly. When we're on the deck, keep your steps light, and follow me.''

Brent muttered something inaudible, and followed Holly up the gangplank.

From the deck, Holly could see the party boat, but there was no sign of Ted Turner. She gave an audible sigh of relief, and motioned toward the cabin. But it wasn't until she saw the cabin door open that warning bells clanged in her head. If Martin Lewis was hiding out, there was no way the door would be open.

Holly raised her gun, and slipped up to the opening. At that same moment, she smelled death, and felt her stomach turn. Within seconds, they were in the salon, staring down at Martin Lewis's lifeless body. She could hear Brent's teeth chattering and his strangled breath as she bent down to check for a pulse. But experience told her she wouldn't find one. The man had been shot through the heart.

"Is he . . . Is he . . . Man, *that* isn't Martin Lewis. . . ."

Brent's words seemed to come to her from afar, even though he stood right beside her.

Their backs were to the salon door, and she heard the *click* before she could answer him. And then the familiar voice. "Nice and easy, now. Put your weapons on the floor."

Holly chanced a glance over her shoulder, and met Ted Turner's evil grin. He was carrying a "Dirty Harry" handgun, and he meant business.

Chapter Eleven

"That's Martin Lewis!" Brent choked out as he placed the gun on the floor in front of him. "But when I saw him, he had hair!"

Holly had already placed her gun on the floor, and held her hands high. "Ted Turner, I presume," she said haughtily. "Or is it Mr. T, or Martin Lewis?"

"It's Martin Teddy Lewis," the man said, motioning for them to sit down. He sneered at Brent. "Thanks for helping me, Brent. I was trying to figure out how to get to the pretty lady when I saw the two of you sneaking on board the *Sweet Alice*."

The man had been wearing a toupee when

Holly had seen him earlier, and now his head was a shiny dome. But he was still wearing the open aloha shirt, revealing his massive chest, and at the moment, he seemed formidable. Holly lowered her arms, and nodded at the body. "That's the man I know as Agent Pearson. So who is he really?"

"Part of the opposing team. A mental pygmy who thought he could take the diamonds right out from under my nose."

"And Ric Brown?"

"His partner. It wasn't bad enough they had to kill a couple of cops. Oh, no, they had to blow the whole thing by getting anxious."

Holly asked, "Then they were a part of your 'team' in the beginning?"

"They were, but I'd never met them personally. They were just a couple of hired guns who were supposed to follow Brent and his sister to Hawaii, and keep them under surveillance until I could get here. But like I said, they got greedy. And trigger happy. They weren't supposed to kill anybody."

Holly tried to sort it out, but finally had to ask, "So, Ric killed Anita, and you killed Ric. That sounds like you were trigger happy, too."

Martin Lewis shrugged. "He was loose with the gun, and it was either him or me."

Holly made a feeble attempt to reason with him. "You obviously have all the diamonds, Mr. Lewis, so what do you want with us?"

"I have all the diamonds except one, and I have the feeling you either have it, or know where it is."

Brent opened his mouth, but before he could speak, Holly said, "I have no idea what you're talking about."

He grinned at Brent. "So, you didn't tell her about that pretty little diamond that's worth a bundle of bucks. That tells me you have it, and were planning to keep it for yourself."

From where Holly was sitting, she could see the *Sea Breeze,* and the flurry of activity. Martin Lewis had his back to the portholes on that side of the boat, and she quickly lowered her eyes. The man's back was to the salon door, too, and it was still open. All she had to do was stall for time.

"I know about the diamond," she said coolly. "I was the one who found it."

Martin Lewis raised a brow. "So you decided to keep it for yourself."

His comment brought a smile to her face.

"I'm a private investigator, Mr. Lewis, and I'm married to a DEA agent. You remember my husband, don't you?"

His eyes narrowed over her, and for the first time, he looked distressed. "You don't look like no P.I., and he didn't look like no fed."

"That just shows you how much looks can be deceiving. For example, up until a few minutes ago, I thought you were a retired business executive, enjoying island life on his party boat."

"Party boat?"

"Sure. Don't you remember? You were having a party on board your boat the day the cops asked you all those questions about Anita. Pretty *wahines* mostly. Did you pay them to play the part?"

His mouth turned down. "So I was having a little party. Big deal. Those ladies were on board because they wanted to be."

Out of the corner of her eye, Holly could see Logan, Al, Danny, and several cops approaching the door. Praying Brent wouldn't inadvertently give them away, she managed a smile. "Well, I suppose I can understand that. You're an attractive man, and you obviously have money."

Her comment took him by surprise, and he actually blushed. "Yeah, well, I've always had a way with the ladies."

"I can tell," Holly said, getting to her feet. She batted her eyelashes, and gave him a dimpled grin. And it was enough to draw his undivided attention.

In that split second, while he was trying to decide if she was coming on to him, Logan stepped up behind him, and shoved a gun in his back. Seconds later, the salon was full of cops, and the nightmare was over.

After Martin Lewis and Brent had been taken away, Logan gave her a healthy shake, and a lengthy hug. "That was really dumb, Holly. You could have been killed!"

Accepting his welcome embrace, Holly looked up at him with a grin. "I'd like to have a dollar for every time you've said that to me."

"Yeah, well I'd like to have a dollar for every time I'm going to say it to you. Thirty or forty years of marriage? Bet I'll be a millionaire."

"You already are," Holly teased. "So, shall we call a truce?"

Logan returned, "I think we'd better if we plan to survive the evening. We're going to be overrun with feds who'll claim we took the case right out from under them, we'll have to face Tutu when she hears about Tonoa, and we'll have to answer a bezillion questions. Think you can handle all that?'' He shook his head, and kissed her softly across her nose. ''Strike that. I learned a long time ago you can handle anything if you put your mind to it.''

Holly gave him a giant hug. ''And that's why we make such a terrific team.''

Logan reached down and picked up the guns off the floor. ''You actually gave Brent my nine-millimeter longslide?''

Holly rolled her eyes. ''I didn't *give* it to him. I *loaned* it to him. . . . Logan . . . Well, I didn't exactly promise Brent anything, but I told him it might help his case if he helped me. He's done some bad things, but he isn't really bad, if you know what I mean.''

Logan's smile was warm, and full of love. ''I know what you mean, sweetheart. Don't forget, your compassion is one of the reasons why I married you.''

Holly snuggled close. ''I want to hear about the other reasons.''

He tweaked her nose. ''I'm afraid you'll have to wait until we're officially on our vacation. Of course, by then, I might have to show you.''

''I can hardly wait,'' she said softly, taking his hand. . . .

''Have you ever seen such a beautiful moon?'' Holly asked, resting her head against Logan's shoulder. They were standing on the veranda, and the soft, fragrant scent of the island promised only peace and tranquility. Cindy and Danny were on the *Sea Breeze*, Tutu and Tonoa were in the kitchen attempting to clean up the mess, and Stump was walking Lila home. It was the end of an incredible day, and love was in the air.

''Not as beautiful as you are,'' Logan said, wrapping an arm around her. ''Does it bother you that Brent is going to have to do some time?''

''No, not really. I know he has to be punished.''

''Well, he's headed in the right direction,'' Logan said gently.

''Speaking of being headed in the right direction, do you think Tutu got through to Tonoa? Or was she wasting her breath?''

''You mean, did he accept the fact she wants

only a friendly relationship? Or that he'd better keep his temper in check if he wants to keep his job?''

''That's a yes on both counts,'' Holly returned.

''Well, he looked like he was eating humble pie during dinner, so I suppose—''

At that moment, a crash sounded from the kitchen, and it sent Holly and Logan running. But when they reached the doorway, they stopped and backed away. Tutu had only dropped a tray of pots and pans, and Tonoa was picking them up.

Holly squeezed Logan's hand. ''Rule number one when you want to make points with the ladies. Come to their aid whenever possible, and do it with a smile on your face.''

Logan returned, ''Hmm, well, I came to your aid lots of times this past year. How many points do I have?''

Holly poked him in the ribs, and ran down the stairs, taunting him to come after her. She knew he would, and she had only one destination in mind. The white sandy beach, where the soft breeze whispered of love.